THE METAL DOOM

By
DAVID H. KELLER, M. D.

I0617077

ARMCHAIR FICTION
PO Box 4369, Medford, Oregon 97504

*For more information about Armchair Books and products, visit our
website at…*

www.armchairfiction.com

Or email us at…

armchairfiction@yahoo.com

IMAGINE A WORLD WITHOUT METAL!

When all the metal was gone, the civilized world ended. People like the Hublers and John Stafford started the slow rebuilding of society—a job made difficult enough by the lack of metal tools and weapons. But there were others trapped in the "new" stone age—roving bands of marauders who relished the new barbarism and whose only drive was to steal or destroy whatever ground the "builders" had regained!

This memorable science fiction classic is a sprawling tale of an Earth gone awry. It is a brilliant, thought-provoking novel that deals with a terrifying premise—the possibility that one day the civilized world might crumble from an incredible new "disease." A disease that could transform all of the world's metal into fine red rust!

FOR A COMPLETE SECOND NOVEL, TURN TO PAGE 131

CAST OF CHARACTERS

PAUL HUBLER
Just an average guy eking out life in the big city. Little did he know that a broken watch was a signal of a world apocalypse.

JOHN STAFFORD
A world without metal was no problem for him. His olden ways and ideas made him a perfect leader in the new Stone Age.

RUTH HUBLER
She loved city life and everything that went with it. Would she be able to survive as a woman in a Stone Age countryside?

ANDREW MACKSON
His dream was the formation of a vibrant, new republic in the area that used to be known as the United States of America.

DR. PERNO
Strong-willed and more courageous than most men, her independent nature was just what the doctor ordered.

ANTHONY BURKE
He placed himself in a fortress of solitude high atop a mountain in hopes of finding a cure for the Metal Doom.

ANGELICA
She was just a kid. How could she be expected to survive in a new world ravaged by outlaw hordes and savage animals?

FOREWORD

Science Fiction has foretold in a hundred different ways the destruction of present civilization. Mankind has had to fight for existence against gigantic life of unusual and unheard of forms originating not only on our own earth but also on other planets. Every conceivable form of physical disaster has wiped out humanity in imagination.

As a matter of historical fact, the human race has survived. Decimated by changes in climate, devoured by gigantic beasts, wiped away by plague and tidal waves, men have survived; and this ability to carry on the torch of life and light the dark places with the spark of civilization has been due, more than anything else, to their possessing the psychological trait of adaptability.

There is no doubt that great disasters will sweep over the world in the centuries to come. Perhaps many of these debacles will be composed of elements peculiarly strange to human experience. Man may die by the millions, but ultimately he will adapt himself to the new conditions of life, make a new adjustment, and once again show that he is the master of the world.

For it does not matter so much to a man what comes into his life as how he reacts to it. It is believed that always there will be enough persons showing a courageous and intelligent reaction to a world disaster to finally save the existence of the human race and enable it to swing back to normal.

It is this thought that prompts the writing of THE METAL DOOM.

David H. Keller, M.D.

It was a peculiar exodus. At the beginning of the debacle, there had been one automobile for every three of the population. One in a million walked for the pleasure of it; the rest rode. Now the only way to leave the city was on foot.

CHAPTER ONE
The Old Watch

"THIS watch cannot be repaired," bluntly stated the watch expert.

"That is a rather odd statement to make. I thought the firm of Cadawalter and Sons stated they could repair any kind of watch or clock ever made."

"Exactly what we have advertised for over a century, but this watch is past repairing. Look at it yourself through this magnifying glass."

Hubler did as he was told. At last he handed the watch back.

"The entire works seem to be badly rusted," was his short comment.

"Exactly. You must have dropped it in some water."

Hubler put the old watch back in his pocket, and started to leave the store. At the door he changed his mind and came back.

"Can you rebuild it?" he asked.

"Perhaps, but cannot promise when."

"Then I'll leave it. It has been a good watch. My grandfather bought it in 1851. You saw it was one of the old key-winding type. We have always kept it in the best of condition. I really prize it highly."

"We'll do the best we can, sir," said the man wearily. This watch business was getting on his nerves. He took the watch and went to the office of the president of the company.

"Here is one more watch, Mr. Cadawalter," was his tired comment.

"Just like all the others?"

"The same condition in all of them, and they're being brought in faster than we can handle them. If the other jewelers in the city are having the same rush we are having, half of the watches in the city must be out of order."

"The only advice I can give you at present is to engage more repairers."

"That would not help. We have no parts to make the repairs with."

"What do you mean?"

"Just that. Every piece of metal in our repair rooms is showing the same red rust that these watches are showing. We have wired and phoned to the wholesalers, and they can't help us. They're having the same trouble."

"Then try to sell the customers watches out of our stock."

"That would be useless. Not one of our new watches are worth a cent. The works in all of them are done for."

"I'll show you one watch that's okay," cried Cadawalter, as he pulled his own watch from his vest. He looked at it, first angrily, then puzzled.

"The blame thing has stopped!" was his comment.

"Of course," countered the repairman. "The same thing has happened to your watch that has happened, or is going to happen, to all the watches."

The rich jeweler opened the back of the case of his watch, spread a piece of white writing paper on his desk and gently shook the watch above it. A fine red dust settled on the paper.

"It's the humidity. There has been a lot of rain this summer," he explained to his employee. "I'm going to give this my personal attention."

He started to telephone, thought better of it, put on his hat and left the office. In the next six hours he visited twelve of the largest jewelry stores in New York City. All told the same story; an unprecedented number of watches being brought in for repairs, no repairs possible because of the lack of repair material, and an inability of the manufacturers to furnish new material.

"And let me show you something else," said the last man he visited. "Here is a bar pin, platinum and diamonds. Yesterday it was worth at least fifty thousand dollars. Look at it under the glass. The metal is gone. Go ahead and break it. Have you examined your jewelry? You better. We're keeping this quiet, but I will tell you confidentially that all of our precious metals are just—I hardly know what word to use, but the word that comes to me is something worse than rust—it's *dry rot.*"

"That is bad," whispered Cadawalter.

"It is worse than bad. It's bankruptcy."

"Have you tried to explain it?"

"No. It's something that's too new. Take the watch business. Yesterday we were doing our usual business, about a hundred a day in for repairs. This morning so many were brought in that we had to close the window. Our spare parts went bad over night. We found our new watches just as bad. I said to myself, 'If steel goes to pieces this way, what is happening to the other metals?' and it didn't take long to find out what was going on in our safes and show cases. The watches just showed the condition early because their parts were so delicate, but even our solid silver looks sick."

Cadawalter closed his eyes as he replied.

"Do you suppose," he asked, as though in a dream, "that the same condition affecting the hair spring of a watch would ultimately affect the suspension cables of a bridge?"

CHAPTER TWO
The Hubler Home

Paul Hubler, his day's work over, decided to walk home. He often walked, preferring it to the intolerable situations of the subway. This evening he was joined by an unusual number of pedestrians, most of them in an angry mood. The subways were having a great difficulty in keeping to their schedules; watches were out of order, block signal systems refused to work; there were strange breaks in the flow of electrical power. As a result it was thought best to discontinue the entire service until a complete investigation and adjustment could be made.

It was not at all satisfactory to the millions of people who had become dependent on this service. It meant late arrival at the supper table, a complete disarrangement of their evening programs.

Everything was wrong anyway. The city dweller had become a slave to time. So many minutes for this and so many for that. Arrive at a place at such a time and leave at such a time. A hundred times a day look at the watch on your wrist or the clock on the tower. How could anyone live when he did not know what time it was?

Paul felt the irritability of the jostling throng, but he did not venture to ask anyone what the trouble was. He just walked home as best he could. He had been rather successful in life and the place he called home was a two-room apartment holding a wife and baby. He smiled as he thought of the baby, almost considered it an adventure in high finance.

In spite of the disaster to his watch, he was completely happy as he swung into the main entrance to the apartment house that contained his home. The fact that a thousand other families lived in that identical beehive gave him no particular concern. But what aroused his interest was a crowd of decidedly angry men and women in front of the elevator door.

"I'm sorry," cried the starter, for the thirtieth time, "but these elevators are out of order, and there is no telling when they'll be running. You'll have to walk."

"Up to the thirtieth floor?" yelled a woman.

"That's just your hard luck," retorted a man, breaking away from the group. "I live on the tenth."

Paul Hubler started to walk up the steps. He lived on the twenty-third floor and even though he was an ardent pedestrian, his muscles ached when he reached that level. He and his wife had lived in this particular apartment over three years and this was the first time he had ever walked up the stairs.

He had a great time in explaining it all to his wife. Ruth Hubler was tired and perhaps a little cross. She was more intent on telling her husband her troubles than in listening to his. The telephone was not working, the electric refrigerator had stopped, the electric stove would not heat. The baby was cross. Nothing but a cold supper could be served, and since the elevator had gone out of commission at noon, she had been unable to go out and buy anything.

Her husband listened to her. Suddenly it occurred to him what it meant to a woman to live on the twenty-third floor under the conditions of the last eight hours.

"We will move," he announced decisively. "We'll go somewhere and live near the ground. It's time to get out of the city anyway. Now that Angelica is walking, we ought to give her a chance. We'll move into the country. That's what we saved the gold for."

From the day they married they had been saving gold pieces. Sometimes a twenty-dollar piece was added to the reserve, but more often a ten or a five. They kept it all in a leather bag, and more than one evening was spent in counting it, arranging it in neat piles.

This evening, without waiting for supper, they opened the leather bag and dumped the gold out on the sitting room table. The man started to pile it, and his wife helped him. The baby in her high chair played with a spoon.

"Look at this two and a half piece, Paul," said the woman. "It seems soft. I can bend it."

And even as she played with it, it broke in two.

At that time Paul Hubler didn't realize what it meant. He was not to blame. Brighter men than he failed to solve the puzzle on the first day. But he did know that something was wrong with their gold and that the gold in the leather bag represented the savings of some years. He hastily put it back in the bag.

"I'm going back to the street," he told his wife, hastily kissing her. "I'm going to exchange all this gold for paper money. What happened to one gold piece might happen to all of them, but if we have paper money we have the government back of us."

He worked until midnight feverishly buying paper money with his gold, losing something at every transaction, but at last ridding himself of all his metal money. On his way home he bought a basket and filled it with food. His legs ached and his brain was tired when he finally reached his apartment at one in the morning. He showed his wife the paper money.

"And it's all worth a hundred cents on the dollar," he explained, "because it has back of it the gold and silver reserve of the nation."

When the Hublers went to bed that night they hoped that everything would be normal the next day. They were sure that during the night the elevators would be repaired, the telephone system put in operation, the electric range and the refrigerator restored to usefulness. They had fully decided to move, but that would take some days. The completeness of the disaster that was slowly overwhelming the nation did not cross the threshold of their consciousness. All they knew was that they had been made most uncomfortable and that by changing their place of residence they might avoid similar occurrences in the future.

Once the morning came it took but a few minutes for Paul and his wife to see that there had been no restoration of service. The telephone was still out of order, the electric servants in their apartment still on strike. There were other petty annoyances. Every safety razor blade in the cabinet was worthless; the kitchen closet was a mess for all the cans had rotted during the night and tomatoes, condensed milk and sardines made a hopeless mixture.

They ate a cold, unsatisfactory breakfast and then the husband started out to see what could be done in regard to moving. At night he slowly climbed up the flights of stairs, hopeless and puzzled, even if not completely defeated. The day's search had brought him some definite information.

Practically all transportation had come to a standstill. The automobiles in the street were silent; the subways and elevated showed no signs of activity. A pushcart here and there carried the goods of an itinerant merchant.

The sun in the sky silently continued its twenty-four hour journey but accurate time had ceased. Not a clock or watch in the city functioned. There was no communication, except by word of mouth. A nation developed anxiety.

CHAPTER THREE
The Hublers Move

"If we move," Paul slowly said to his wife, "we'll have to go on foot. We'll be able to take hardly anything with us. A little bedding and some clothes—and perhaps some books. We'll stay here tonight and tomorrow I'll try and buy some kind of a wagon or push cart. We can make up a few bundles and start up Fifth Avenue. If we keep on going long enough, we'll reach the country."

"But do we have to go?" asked a worried Ruth.

"I believe so. All day I tried to learn what I could. Of course all I could hear were rumors and suspicions. The worst part is the interruption of train service; and the boats have stopped. There is no more food entering the city. There is enough here to feed the people for a week or two, but a lot of it is spoiled like our canned goods. Besides it has to be distributed through the city by hand. We had better get out. We ought to move tonight. Perhaps we can make it if we start. Tomorrow a half a million people may have the same idea; the next day five million. I'm tired but...would you have the courage to start tonight? Let's do it. It will be cooler traveling in the dark."

"We could use the baby carriage," suggested Ruth.

But one look showed that this was a hopeless idea. The springs were broken and rusted. Three hours later the Hublers left their apartment with three compact bundles and Angelica who was just old enough to realize that there was something unusual going on. As they left the apartment Paul closed the door, but it fell to the floor. The hinges had decayed! He showed it to his wife and commented:

"Looks as though we were not leaving a minute too soon."

An hour later they were on Fifth Avenue going north. The street was not crowded, but all the people on it were going north and all carried bundles. Evidently a number of people were going to the country.

At midnight Paul Hubler bought a pushcart from an Armenian. He paid exactly one hundred dollars for that two-wheeled wagon and it held together exactly two days, which was a record. In those two days they were able to make twenty miles. The morning of the third day found them out in the country. True, it was an artificial country made up largely of estates of rich men, but still it was country. They were tired but vaguely happy, exhausted with their unusual exertions; but satisfied they had taken the correct action. They had been able to buy some food. Chickens had been purchased and broiled over a fire.

Fortunately the weather had been warm. There was no rain. Milk could be bought for Angelica. Under other circumstances it might have been a picnic.

After the pushcart broke down, Paul bought a wheelbarrow. He had to use a good deal of rope, and at last a stick for an axle but it kept on going and was large enough to carry the load. The family was tired, but something kept them going. Paul Hubler had an idea in his head, and that idea was slowly becoming dominant. He wanted to get as far away from civilization as he could. At last he pushed the wheelbarrow up an unused country road into the hill country, and there, on the sixth day he found what he was looking for—an abandoned farm. It probably was part of one of the large estates, purchased by a multimillionaire to round out a corner of his holdings and to be promptly forgotten.

The house was an old log house, the space between the logs chinked with mud; part of the roof had started to collapse, but the fireplace and chimney were in good condition. The forest had grown up to the house and there were a lot of fallen branches on the ground.

A spring gushed out of the rocks in back of the house and gurgled noisily across the field.

"We'll live here," announced Paul to his tired wife and crowing baby. "Here we have water, a fireplace, wood and a shelter from the storm. I can repair the roof. Somewhere we can find a source of food. Somehow we'll survive. Millions of people in the cities will die but we'll survive."

"Do you mean that we're going to live here?" asked Ruth.

"Yes. Right here."

"But you always lived in the city!"

"I know. I spent so many hours a day over my bookkeeping...and in exchange for that I was given each week a check. We took that check and bought things, food, light, services, transportation, communication. We paid the rent. Now we'll live here, and most of the things we used to pay for we'll now have for nothing, save the sweat of our brow."

Ruth thought of her pleasant, clean, two-room apartment. She remembered the electric stove, the refrigerator, the little washing machine and her electric iron.

"I don't want to live this way!" she cried. "I must have been over influenced by your arguments. Did we have to leave the city? Surely someone has found out by this time what the trouble was. How about our scientists, our inventors? I don't want to live this way."

Paul took her in his arms, baby and all. He kissed her.

"Some day we may go back to the city," he assured her, as he wiped away her tears. "Some day—but not now."

CHAPTER FOUR
The New Disease

Meanwhile, the nation had not been idle. A thousand scientists, a million technicians, twenty-five million workmen were trying to repair the damage done and find some method of preventing the further destruction of all the metals.

For at the end of the first week it was apparent that some peculiar and new disease was affecting all the metals, not only in the United States but all over the world. The real facts were hard to determine because communication ceased so suddenly, but it was logical to suppose that if a condition affected all steel in one continent it would similarly affect the steel of the world, and that if gold crumbled to nothing in New York, it was doing the same in London and Peking.

Research was active, but lack of communication prevented any concerted effort. The collapse of civilization would have been slower and more orderly had the telephone continued to function. Tremendous differences would have been observed had it been possible to give directions over the radio. But the radio, dependent as it was on metals, broke down as early as the telephone. Thus each scientist fought a lonely fight in his separate laboratory, handicapped by the rapid disintegration of his armamentarium. Glass and porcelain and pottery were unchanged. Everything made of metal rotted, and the finer the piece of metal the more rapid was its decay.

A hundred experts announced a hundred opinions to those who cared to hear them. Some thought it was a rapid form of electrolysis; others favored the theory that another planet had rained bacteria on the earth that lived on metals rather than on organic life. Some advanced thinkers spoke vaguely of a power, like radiant energy, splitting all elements into hydrogen. No one was certain of just what was happening to the metals of the earth, but everyone who had any intelligence was slowly becoming aware of the fact that mankind was slowly losing all benefits derived from the use of metals.

For centuries the advancement of the human race had, to a great extent, depended on the use of metals. Copper, tin, bronze, iron, steel, had been the physical basis on which all progress had been based. Electricity, the great servant of humanity could only serve through channels of metals. The progress of mankind resulted from increasing rapidity of communication and greater ease of transportation and here again metal played a vital part. Muscleman had been replaced by mind—man through the use of machines fabricated of metal. Every useful art, every necessary science depended on the use of metals.

In a few parts of the world mankind was still in the Stone Age, but even here the steel knife was replacing the flint one. During the first weeks of the metal disease no one was able to accurately prophesy what the end was going to be, and even the most brilliant thinkers were unable to communicate their nightmares except to a few scientists in their immediate neighborhood. It was this rapidity of metal destruction, the immediate effect on communication and transportation, that made the entire period such a dreadful one. The nations broke up into states, the states into small units. Towns organized as best they could into defensive units. Each farmhouse became an isolated fort. It soon became a survival of the strongest, everyone for himself and God help the weak and incompetent.

The last census had shown that sixty percent of the nation's population lived in cities. Within two weeks this sixty percent were trying to move into the country, anywhere, just so they could get food. For years the urbanite had read that there was an overproduction of food, that wheat, potatoes, milk, butter, eggs, were always in abundance. They knew that all their food came from the country. What they did not know was the labor necessary to produce this food, and concerning this they were indifferent. They had money and with this money they bought food sent to the cities from the country.

Now the trains, trucks, and boats had ceased to carry the food to the cities. The city men reasoned that the food must still be there, out in the country, so they went out to get it. They had money and they believed that food could still be bought.

It was a peculiar exodus. At the beginning of the debacle, there had been one automobile for every three of the population. One in a million walked for the pleasure of it; the rest rode. Now the only way to leave the city was on foot. Throughout the entire nation there was neither ship, locomotive, automobile nor airplane, capable of transporting humanity singly or in groups. The railroads were rapidly becoming streaks of red rust; motive machinery was rotting, ships were sinking in the harbors.

So the people started to walk out of the cities. As they walked they scattered. For a while they met kindness; their money bought food; the roadside stands did a rushing business. But the demand was greater than the supply and then became a struggle for existence. Those who had food refused to sell it; those who were dying for lack of food tried to steal it. In every farming community for a month around, wars were waged. With clubs and stones the embittered farmers fought for their right to use their supplies, to save their own lives. Except where overwhelmed by sheer weight of numbers, the farmers always won the battle. At the end of the month a slow adjustment had begun. The brighter of the city dwellers began to learn how to survive under the new conditions. Here and there they were welcomed by the farm group, and even started in the country life with as much help as possible.

The death rate was high. Just how many of the total population died during that first month of panic will never be known. Years later the revisited cities revealed horrible stories of suffering. Thousands and hundreds of thousands of people never left the city. After all it was their home; they knew no other life; they could not believe that the city was doomed, and so they remained until it was too late.

Others stayed because it was their duty to do so. The policeman on his beat, the doctor in his hospital, the nurse by her patient, the mother by her infant child remained and died on duty. The full tale of heroism will never be told until the day of Resurrection, but there remained a certain percent of humanity, who died with their faces to the battle rather than yield to the panic that evacuated the cities in surging white-faced mobs.

Thus the cities died. Dependent on metals, they died when metals disappeared. Humanity, changing overnight into the second Stone Age, lost much of its civilization, and all of its congestion. The psychology of the period was peculiar in that such a large part of man's knowledge became suddenly useless, because he had lost the metal tools whereby that knowledge could be expressed and put into practical use. Man entered the second Stone Age with the intelligence of a man and the ability of a child to use that intelligence.

So, in a few months, humanity drifted back into the dawn of time and the beginning of things.

CHAPTER FIVE
Hubler Makes an Ax

The three people started to live in the old log house, and it did not make such an uncomfortable home. A fire was started in the fireplace and never allowed to go out. Potatoes were roasted in the ashes with corn on the cob. An occasional chicken was broiled a piece at a time on the end of a stick, and Angelica became very fond of a nanny goat that had, for no apparent reason, adopted the Hubler family. The goat furnished the baby both milk and a playmate.

The days were very busy. Paul was out all the time gathering sticks, breaking them as best he could, and filling one end of the house with a winter's supply of firewood. At other times he was on the roof with branches of pine and mud, which he spread over the thin spots in an effort to make the house waterproof. He cleaned out the spring, and tried to make the land around the house look clean and orderly. Every day no matter what else he did, he spent some time throwing stones at a target. He forced Ruth to do the same thing. Then one day he began the collection of piles of small stones, near the house.

"We may need them," was his only comment.

During this month he did a lot of thinking. It made his wife rather unhappy to have him sit on the floor near her and keep still for some hours on end.

"Why don't you talk to me," she would ask.

"I have to think about this. I want to find out what it all means," was his invariable reply.

Then one night he started to make his ax. There was a hickory stick, split at one end, a stone, flat but rather sharp at one end, and some pieces of wild grapevine. His first attempt was a failure, and to the average man it would have been disheartening. He simply tried it again, and finally he found how to wrap the twines of grape vine in such a way that they held the stone. Then he started to use the ax and found at once that there was something wrong with the balance of it. The handle was too long.

It was one thing to saw through a piece of hickory and another to cut it off evenly with pieces of stone. Hubler soon found this out, and reverted to the old method of burning the end in the fire, then pounding off the charred end and burning some more and pounding some more until he had managed just the required length. At last he showed the ax to Ruth rather proudly. She did not seem to be too enthusiastic about it.

"What are you going to do with it?" she asked.

He looked at it for some time before he replied.

"It will be a handy thing to kill something with."

"What are you going to kill?"

"Something...anything that needs killing."

After that he spent considerable time every day in swinging the ax around his head and learning to strike with it. In a week he became almost proud of his ability. His muscles were hardening, his coordination improving. He made a smaller one for his wife and encouraged her to use it. He even made a little one for Angelica and it was great sport for the three of them to go out in the warm sunshine of the afternoon and practice with the axes.

"We're going to go slowly back into the arts of the Stone Age," Paul explained. "Of course it will take time, but as the need arises, our ability will grow. It will be interesting to watch our development. We know about the sling, the bow and arrow, the long spear and even the catapult, but we haven't made them for centuries and naturally have never used them. We don't have to invent these things, we simply have to become proficient in the making of them and then in the use of them. We know the theory, the mechanics—what we must learn is the actual construction. When I was a boy, I gathered Indian arrowheads. I can tell you a lot about their shapes, but right now I can't tell how they're made or how they're fastened to the shaft. Someone will have to learn all this. Perhaps the time will come when there will be manufacturing centers where nothing but arrows are made.

"But we have to have these things. The man who gets them first and becomes proficient in their use will be at a great advantage over other men."

"In what way?" asked Ruth, "and why?"

"Because every man may have to fight for his rights?"

"But how about the law? And government?"

"I don't know; but I suspect that law and government have ceased to exist."

"In other words you're telling me that you're planning to kill—and kill, and...why you never killed a chicken."

"I know; but that doesn't say I won't kill—if necessary."

Paul was not psychic, but he did a lot of thinking. As a result he developed the habit of carrying his ax with him on his trips to the wood to gather branches. He was out one day experimenting with the ax on some dead wood when he thought he heard a cry. The next second he was sure of it. It was Ruth and she was in trouble. Ax in hand he started to run home. He ran silently, with sure steps; as he ran he thought to himself that two months before such speed would have winded him; now he was growing tough. He almost jumped around the corner of the house and found what he had expected.

A big man, with ragged clothes and a long beard, had Ruth in his arms trying to kill her. She was scratching, and biting and kicking. Angelica, sitting against the side of the house was just crying.

Paul, almost automatically, swung the ax around and brought the sharp edge of the stone down on the man's head. He was rather surprised to see how easy it was to hit a man like that and how very efficacious it was. The man just grunted and dropped and that was all there was to it.

Ruth started to faint, thought better of it, picked up the little child and started to comfort her.

"Thanks, Paul," she said, simply. "Now I guess I'll go and cook something for supper and you can tidy up the yard."

Hubler turned the man over on his back. There was no doubt about the fact that he was dead. So he dragged him over to a little gully and piled a lot of stone over him.

"And that's Number One," he said out loud, "and the rest that come will get the same treatment, and tomorrow I'm going to start in earnest to make a bow and some arrows, because the next man may have a club or an ax and I'm not sure how I would do in a real fight. It's one thing to hit a man in the back of the head and another thing to hit him between the eyes. But one thing is sure. So long as I live here I'm going to take care of Ruth and Angelica. No tramp or common bum is going to hurt them so long as I can prevent it—and I have a feeling that I can prevent it so long as I'm alive."

After supper Ruth took her ax and went to the edge of the woods.

"I'm going to learn to throw this ax," she explained to her husband. "I'm going to learn to throw it so it will hit a tree and cut its way into the bark."

"That's the way we used to throw a pen knife when I was a boy," commented her husband. "We threw it all different ways in a game called mumble-le-peg."

"This is not a game, and a woman does not always hit what she aims at," replied Ruth, "so you and the baby get out of the way."

For a while she did not even touch the tree. Then she was always able to hit it with some part of her ax. After two hours, just at the end of twilight, she had the satisfaction of seeing the stone edge of the ax sink into the bark.

"I'll do better tomorrow," she said, "and in a week or two I'll be about perfect."

Later in the evening they sat before the fire. The night wasn't cold but there was a chill in the air that told of the approaching fall. Angelica was asleep on her fragrant bed of pine needles.

"How do you feel about it all, Paul?" the woman asked.

"Fine as can be."

"I mean about killing that man?"

"It's all right. He had to be killed. Of course, he was the first one, but there always has to be a first one of everything. And if I hadn't killed him he would have killed me. I have a feeling that I'm going to kill more men before things reach normal, and all I want to do is to always feel that I'm justified in the killing. I never want to kill just for the pleasure of it."

As he talked he was pushing a sharp stone backward and forward in a line across the handle of the ax.

"What are you doing that for, Paul?"

"That's my tally."

CHAPTER SIX
The First Visitor

Two days after that, in the afternoon, the family was out on the edge of the forest practicing ax throwing. Even Angelica was toddling around throwing little sticks at rocks.

Ruth took careful aim and hit a tree in a perfect throw.

"That's fine," exclaimed a voice, "but I wish you wouldn't pick out a sugar maple to practice on."

Hubler whirled around, ax in hand, ready to fight.

But the young man, smiling, advanced with hands above his head.

"Don't take me too seriously, my dear sir. I have only come to call on you and your wife."

"We do not want any callers. A man called a few days ago and he is under the rocks in the ravine."

"You persist in misunderstanding me. My name is John Stafford. I own a few thousand acres of land around here. In fact, I own this farm, though I never visited it until today; but one of my men told me he had seen smoke from the chimney so I thought I'd walk over and see who was here. Have you been here long?"

"We have," answered Ruth. "Ever since we left the city when the metals went to pieces. We came right here, and tried to get along. There is still some money in our pocket and if you tell us what the rent is, we'll be glad to pay it and stay. We like it here. We hoped that we could plan our life so we could live here."

"In an age of stone?" asked Stafford.

"That's what it looks like," asserted Hubler, slightly smiling, as he looked at his ax. "Would you mind going to the house? We're sorry we can't offer you something worth while in the shape of food, but the spring water is excellent."

Later on the visitor restarted the conversation.

"So you folks left New York early?"

"Very early. We were in the first rush, and, as I had a pushcart and later on a wheelbarrow, we made rather good time, in spite of the baby. You see I had always prided myself on being a pedestrian and my ability to walk came in good stead. I reasoned that there were a lot of people behind us and that most of them would stay on the cement roads, so at the first good chance, I hit a dirt one and landed here. So far we've only had two visitors, and the first one did not live very long. He was rough with Ruth. You're number two."

"I think," said Stafford, "that you are the kind of people I'm looking for. Let me tell you my story. I've always been rich, a manufacturer, but my main interest was in horses and the olden days and the way folks used to do things. People thought I was a fool, and I guess I was. For example, I hated barbed wire. Not an inch of it is on my stock farm. Stone fences and rail fences, but not a bit of metal, not even a nail in them. Same way with my house. All built of wood, put together with wooden nails. I even had a set of wooden dishes. I collected arrowheads, learned to shoot with a bow. I have as fine a collection of tomahawks as you ever saw. And horses! You ought to see those horses.

"Then the crash came. I was in New York at the time. I waited for a while longer than you did, just long enough to arrive at an opinion of the seriousness of it all and then I went up the river in a sailboat, though part of the time I had to drift around waiting for the wind. But I arrived before much of the mob came, and then I started to save my place.

"Guess how I did it? I just stood at my front gate and gave away money. I always had a lot of cash in the house and now I gave it away. For everyone who came by, I told them I was sorry for them and here was a twenty dollar bill or a ten dollar gold piece and they should go on to the next town. I had my hostlers and housemen in back of me with clubs. We were a bad looking lot and so the mob flowed on past my place. Lots of my neighbors had a bad time. Some were killed and some came to my place for safety, but we got by. Not a horse was stolen; not a fence was broken."

"I suppose the money you gave them was worthless," commented Hubler.

"Certainly. I knew it when I gave it to them...but they didn't.

"Of course we don't know for sure, but I think the United States is a thing of the past. Even the state government is gone. But I rule. I *am* the state. I've fenced in three thousand acres of land and that land I *am* going to hold, and the things on it are going to stay mine. My friends and I are going to live on it, in a new stone age, and we're going to work out our salvation and perhaps do a little to save other communities, and anyone who is against us is going to die."

"So you came here because you heard we had squatted on your land and burned some of your wood and killed a stray hen or two?" asked Paul Hubler, tightening his grip on his ax.

The visitor laughed, as he answered:

"No. I came here because I heard there was a man and woman and little baby trying to solve their problems in an intelligent manner. To be honest, we've been watching you for several weeks. I've been pleased with the reports of my men. I think that you are the type of man we're looking for. You're brave, moral, and you have not only imagination but also some ability. In our life we need men like you. I'm not going to ask you to come and live with us, though someday you may want to, but I do want you to come over and see us and get an idea of our plans. Perhaps we can give you some supplies to help you over the winter and my men can come over and fix that roof up for you and help build a pen for the goat, and in addition you ought to have a horse.

"You come and see me and talk over plans with me. Let me help you. Then, if the pinch comes and you need more help, you know where to go. It's not so bad now, but when winter comes, these woods will be dangerous for a lone man and his family. I believe there will be gangs of men, hungry and desperate, who will comb over the state this winter like packs of wolves. If you're with us, your wife and baby would be safe."

"There is something to that," replied Hubler, thoughtfully.

"Think it over," urged the visitor. "Let me draw a map for you in this dirt. Here is your road and here is another road and that comes out on the concrete, and then turn to the left and my place is just around the bend of the road. You can't miss it. Only be careful when you come near to the fences. I have sentries out now and we tell the people to move on or get killed...and we mean it. If one of the men says anything to you simply say, *"Better days are coming"* and that will pass you through the lines, but I'll tell the boys to be on the lookout for a man with a pretty baby. We'll have to make a bone necklace for that little one."

"Do you really think there's going to be trouble, Mr. Stafford?" whispered Ruth, holding Angelica a little tighter in her arms.

"Positive of it. We have had bad days and worse are on their way. The cities literally vomited their people. For a while the crooks stayed on to steal but they soon saw that their plunder would not feed them, so they joined the mob. And the way we've had to treat them is not very nice to think about."

"But I'm sure there were some nice people you could have helped," insisted Ruth. "There must have been some nice people who passed your place."

"There were some," agreed Stafford. "In fact I have ten families on my place now. But you would be surprised what a very few there were that I could feel sure of—enough to ask them to join my new republic. It was this way—I had an idea, and if they were ever so nice and did not harmonize with that idea, I simply could not help them."

"What was the idea?" interrupted Hubler.

"You ought to know it from the fact that I have asked you to join me. I'm forming a colony; its isolation is just as complete as though it was on a desert island in the Pacific. It's going to be composed of separate families of clean-cut young men and women who are intelligent and courageous and who have imagination. I want every unit to become self-sustaining, but at the same time every man and every woman should be able to contribute something in the way of a specialty that will tend toward the public welfare. For example there must be a doctor who is able to do surgery, an engineer who is able to construct fortifications and help us with our artillery, an expert in agriculture who will advise us in the growing and harvesting of crops. There must be an expert in pottery, someone who can teach the women to harvest the flax and cotton and spin thread and weave cloth. There will have to be a great deal of cottage industry. The time may come when we'll be able to have men and women work just at one task, but for the time being I want every man and woman to learn to do everything. But above all they have to be brave—have a vision of the future, learn to prepare for that future."

"It sounds interesting," admitted Ruth.

"But it does not explain why you picked us out," added Paul.

"I thought you would see," answered Stafford. "You left the city early. That shows foresight…imagination. You had a quick conception of what was going to happen. You realized that safety lay in isolation, and you saw that most of the people would be afraid to leave the cement roads.

"You came here. The two of you took a deserted farm and broken down house and made a home. You learned to do things. I bet that right now you're sowing seed corn for next year, and you have set aside the winter's firewood. You made your axes and started to learn how to use them. You're taking good care of the baby. The place looks clean. You three are a family. If you never saw anyone for five years you would get along. That all shows you're adaptable. I want you. I wish I had fifty families like your family. Will you join us?"

The man and woman looked at each other. They understood.

"Not just now," answered Hubler. "We have really had a good deal of pleasure out of this experience. We have sort of made a second honeymoon out of it. I think that we would like to stay here this winter—at least try it. Perhaps in the spring we'll join you. The baby will be older then and should have the company of other children. Of course, something may happen and then we'll be glad to come. It was kind of you to praise us the way you have, and invite us, but just now we want to try things out a little longer."

The visitor rose and stretched himself.

"I will send you some things," he said, "a few things to make you more comfortable, and I'll have my scouts drop in now and then. Any time you change your mind, come over and join us."

CHAPTER SEVEN
News from the North

John Stafford walked down to the road, mounted his horse and was soon around the turn of the road. Paul and Ruth waved a gay goodbye to him and then, calling Angelica, went into their home.

"That's a nice man," commented Ruth. "I wonder if he's married."

"At least he has an idea of the important part women are going to play in the new world," laughed her husband.

On the way back to his farm Stafford did a lot of thinking, and the end of the thinking was the same as the beginning, and that was the fixed idea that Paul and Ruth and Angelica Hubler would make a valuable addition to the new social order he hoped to establish.

He was a little surprised to find a strange horse hitched to a post in front of his home, and the rider of this horse serenely seated on a chair on the front gallery. The newcomer lost no time in introducing himself.

"I'm Andrew Mackson, Mr. Stafford. I'm from Vermont, and I'm hunting *men.*"

"Do you mean real men, Mr. Mackson?"

"Nothing but that kind."

"I have a number on this farm. What can we do for you?"

"Have you the time to listen to me?"

"Certainly. After that we can have supper. I'll have your horse put up. Looks like a fast animal."

"He is. But I don't want to impose upon your hospitality. Still, if you insist, I will stay. Roads are dangerous. I judge you're fond of horses?"

"But part of my life."

"How are you shoeing them nowadays?"

"Oh! Just leather pads securely tied with thongs. On dirt roads I don't worry about shoes. My horses are doing well."

"How about fences?"

"Some," Stafford answered, "mainly of stone."

"There are lots of stones where I'm from. But let me tell you why I'm here. My part of Vermont is just about deserted, but it has more pretty, small farms than you ever dreamed of, and lots of waterpower. Just lots of timber, and most of the farms have stone houses on them. I want men and women to come up there and live. I can show them how to build mills to run with waterpower, and we can grind the grain with millstones. I think that some day we can even get some timber out, if we can make a saw with flint teeth. It's nice country up there, and we have worlds of the very thing you need in this new life."

"What's that?"

"Stone. We have stones of every kind and every shape. What ever you want in the way of stone, we have it. Add to that waterpower and forests, and stone houses already built, and you have a paradise. All we need I have mentioned. We want men and women and children. People with courage and imagination and the determination to do everything in their power to help build up a new civilization. Do you know any that way?"

"That's the kind *I'm* hunting for, Mr. Mackson. You may not know it, but right here is the capital of the new republic. Just as soon as I can find them, I'm going to put a hundred families here and we're going to work our new life out together. We're going to have a stone age here that will be more worthwhile than any metal age ever dreamed of being."

"You wouldn't want to spare any of the families you have?"

"Not one. The kind of family I'm looking for is scarce."

Mackson drummed on the seat of the empty chair by his side. At last he broke the silence.

"I've just thought of something, Mr. Stafford. Up in Vermont I have an idea of a small unit of people who will form a small commonwealth and be absolutely independent of the rest of the world. Independently you arrived at the same idea. Down in Connecticut I found the beginnings of another unit and the leader there talked the same as we talked. He wanted to show the world that the Yankees could do more with stone than had ever been thought of. He asked me to bring my folks down and learn how to really use stone—just as if he could teach a Vermonter anything about stone.

"My idea is this. In the old days of metal and electricity, there were a lot of no-account people; just a lot of them who thought of nothing except their own pleasure and never had an original idea from the day they were born to the day they died. But at the same time, here and there all over the states, there were worthwhile folk, perhaps descendants of the old pioneers, at least men and women with lots of stone in their backbones— folks who never knew when they were licked.

"Those people here and there are going to work along the same lines. Use all the intelligence they have and work out their own problems in their own way. These colonies are going to be like an oasis in the desert. The common herd will mill around and finally die out. Perhaps a good many will have to be killed. Finally only the people in the colonies will be left. And then we'll have to unite in some way, formulate a defense, if for nothing else. Perhaps we can build a large fort somewhere, so if we care to attack we can use that for a rallying place. I don't want to leave Vermont and you don't want to leave New York but we might have to anyhow."

"You mean there might be a war?"

"Certainly."

"Whom with?"

"I don't know; but someone. There are a lot of people in South America, and there is Asia. We won't know for a long time what happened in Asia, but they probably felt the change less there than we did. But, no matter whom we fight, we *will* have a war, and we might as well get ready. My young men are out every day shooting at targets with their bows and arrows, and we're working at catapults that will throw a twenty-pound stone a hundred yards. We're going to hunt wild pigs this winter with stone-tipped lances, from horseback. Now if you want sport, try that."

Stafford ignored the sporting side of the conversation and returned to the serious part.

"So you think there might be trouble. I think so, too. In fact I think we'll have a little war this winter. There are several gangs of New Yorkers working around here, and they aren't pleasant neighbors. When winter comes they're going to be hungry and my people are going to have food. I've been thinking of building a fort, so the women and children will be safe."

"Might be a good idea," commented Mackson, "but I tell you what I think. As soon as winter comes, at least cold weather, put your men on horseback, and round them up. Give the rascals so many hours to get out and stay out. If they start to fight, exterminate them. After you wipe out a few of the gangs, the others will give you a wide berth. There were some men like those you mentioned that came down from Montreal, hunting for warmer climate, and believe me, they found it when we started after them. A fort is all right, but if you fight early enough and hard enough, you won't need one."

CHAPTER EIGHT
The New Republic

The conversation between the two leaders was interrupted by supper. After that there were more conferences, the result of which a very important decision was reached. The former area of the United States was divided into five parts, and only one dividing line was artificial. The parts were 1 and 2, east of the Appalachian and north and south of the old Mason and Dixon line; 3, between the Appalachian and the Mississippi; 4, between the Mississippi and the Rockies, and 5, west of the Rockies. Each of these five parts were to be absolutely independent of the other four but were to unite for defense. Within each part were to be formed a number of separate, independent communities, who would stay in communication and help each other in every way possible. Once a year representatives of the smaller units would meet. Once every five years there would be a meeting at or near St. Louis of five representatives of the five republics.

That was the program formulated during the evening's conference. It avoided all finances, for it was early recognized that money, as a means of exchange, was something that would have to be developed. The exchange of work and the exchange of surplus commodities, the ancient system of barter, for many years would replace money. Within each community each citizen would contribute toward the welfare of the community and in return would be cared for by the community.

One of the men engaged in the conference objected:

"That's socialism, pure and simple. No community, founded on those lines, has ever survived. It does away with personal initiative."

Stafford's argument was brief.

"None of those communities lived in the Stone Age."

Stafford turned to Mackson:

"You're a pretty good talker, Mr. Mackson. Someone has to carry the message. How would you like to give a few years of your life to the spreading of this political gospel? I'll loan you a few of my best men to serve as a bodyguard, and you can go out to the Pacific Coast and see how far you can get in organizing the old U. S. A. along these lines. Someone has to do it. Every place where they share the vision of the future that we have, talk things over and see if you can get them to sign on the dotted line. When you reach the coast, have one of their big men ride back with you, so he can become personally acquainted with the situation in the east. Will you do it?

"That's a big contract, Mr. Stafford."

"But I'm asking a big man. Your only reason for refusing would be your honest conviction that your Vermont colony would go to pieces in your absence."

"It wouldn't," the Vermont man was honest enough to admit, "for my brother up there is really a better man than I am."

"Then it's all settled. I have a piece of paper here and a quill pen. I'll draw up articles of confederation, and you and I will head the list of signators. You take the paper with you. I have a feeling that in this room we're making history, gentlemen. It may be that some day this paper will rank in importance with the Magna Carta and the Declaration of Independence. How shall I start it? Something like this:

WE, THE UNDERSIGNED LEADERS OF NEW ECONOMIC AND POLITICAL GROUPS WITHIN THE BOUNDARIES OF THE UNITED STATES, BUT EXISTING UNDER A NEW STONE AGE, BROUGHT ABOUT BY THE METAL DOOM, DO HEREBY PLEDGE OURSELVES TO THE FORMATION OF A CONFEDERATION OF THESE GROUPS FOR THE FOLLOWING REASONS:

That was the way the first rough copy started. It was rewritten several times, but at last they had something that satisfied the group of educated men gathered in the great livingroom.

Arrangements were made for the little group of men to start west early the next morning. The four men selected to go with Mackson were all experienced horsemen and expert marksmen with the bow and arrow. There was no reason to think that there would be any special danger, but it was felt best to be prepared. The five men realized that even with the best of luck it would be more than a year before they returned to their homes. At the same time the novelty of the journey was such that they looked forward to it with a spirit of enthusiasm.

Later on, when communication became better, other colonies claimed that they were the first to originate a plan for a new confederation. They deserve honor for their originality but as far as historical research is concerned it's practically certain that the honor of priority fell to Stafford and Mackson and it's the paper that Mackson carried to the Pacific Ocean and back to Vermont that is recognized as the greatest paper of the new Stone Age. The names of signers on it comprise practically all of the great men of the new world, three of the signers later becoming Presidents.

Stafford made the final comment as the meeting adjourned:

"Tell those you meet, Mackson, that this first and foremost is a survival of the fittest. Those who cannot be trusted, who are incompetent to learn the new lesson, who hold on to the old ideas of power and riches and the oppression of the poor must be cast out of our communities. If they perish, they perish. We dare not try to save them. The same way with the feeble-minded, the insane and the degenerate. Our society must not save them."

CHAPTER NINE
How One Man Died

It is certain that since the discovery of printing, no world disaster had ever been so poorly documented as the period of *The Metal Doom*. Practically overnight there was a more or less complete cessation of the daily press. One day the giant presses of the country were stamping the news on thousands of tons of pulp paper; the next day those same presses were silenced. One day news was flashed from the Orient to the Occident in the winking of an eye; the next day the telephone, telegraph and wireless had ceased to serve mankind.

Time passed and eventually the scientists had some fairly definite idea of how humanity had reacted to the new conditions under which life had to be lived. An interesting and perhaps partly accurate history could be written, but at best only the surface of fact would be scratched; most of the reactions can only be guessed at.

One man, however, laboriously wrote his story before he died, and because that story tells the tale of a brave man, and also because it partly explains the final statement of Stafford, it is worthwhile adding that story to this tale.

At the onset of THE METAL DOOM, humanity was probably as kindly foolish towards its delinquents and abnormals, as it had ever been in any historical epoch. In the United States alone there were over a half million criminals being supported by the taxpayers and another half million abnormals composed of the insane, epileptic, and mentally deficient members of society. Whereas other ages constantly eliminated the unfit, there was, in the United States, a determined effort to prolong the life of each person as long as possible, irrespective of his ability to provide for himself or the impossibility of improvement or ultimate cure. The highest type of the medical profession believed that the prolongation of a human life even ten minutes was worth the expenditure of every possible scientific effort.

Consequently, the abnormals were placed in special hospitals and cared for in such large numbers that their maintenance became a most serious problem to the taxpayer. At least as much was spent in the care of the physically defective each year as was spent in all forms of education. Irrespective of the number of hospitals built each year, the demand for more beds always kept ahead of the building program.

To these prisons and hospitals the Metal Doom came. The prisons constituted a permanent menace to the new social order. Capital punishment had been almost completely abolished and life imprisonment substituted in its place. Thousands and hundreds of thousands of degenerate criminals were held in restraint only by steel bars and modern firearms. Overnight the firearms became useless. Within a week the steel bars decayed and these criminals, frantic with fear, desperate with hunger and menacing from the possibility of complete revenge upon society, hurled themselves on a world that was already staggering to its social debacle. Ultimately decent society eliminated these criminals in many a hard fought and bloody battle, but for some years gangs of law violators roamed the forests and swallowed all who came within their clutch.

With the insane and feebleminded, the problem was a different one. Probably the solution was slightly different in each hospital. Apparently the majority of superintendents felt that all they could do was to liberate their patients and allow them the right to survive if they could.

Dr. Hiram Jones was the medical Director of the Central Pennsylvania State Hospital for the Mentally Defective. His patients were probably lower in intelligence than any similar institution in the United States. There was a larger percentage of idiots and low-grade imbeciles. Dr. Jones, in his daily rounds, preached the gospel of loving kindness and the prolongation of every life. He sometimes wondered just why his helpless charges should be allowed to live, but he never wavered from his professional pride in their care. In his more grandiose moments he called them all his children, certainly a large and peculiar family, thirteen hundred idiots and near idiots.

His superior officer was a political appointee, who, when the crash came, left at once, to take care of himself and his family. Of the one hundred and ninety employees, a large number walked off when they realized the impossibility of caring for their charges under the new condition.

Dr. Jones and ten faithful men and women tried for two days to feed and care for the thirteen hundred patients. During that time Jones went without sleep. At twilight of the second day he had arrived at a decision. He gave orders that all of the little ones should be put to bed. This was not a difficult task. Going to bed and to sleep was something that all in the hospital had done so often that it had become routine.

Sleep and quiet, blessed twin angels, hovered over the hospital, and then Dr. Hiram Jones started to make his last round. He paused at each bed, and with a medicine dropper carefully placed between parted lips five drops of medicine and then on to the next bed. He worked methodically and quickly, aided by his little band of nurses. At last all of the patients were asleep.

And from that sleep we trust they wakened into a world where all little children are bright and happy and intelligent.

Dr. Hiram Jones said goodbye to his nurses and advised them to do what seemed best to them and then he went to his office. There he lit a tallow candle and finished writing his story. He used a quill pen he had just made for the purpose. He had written the story of those hard days and now he added an ending as though to justify himself in the eyes of all who would come after him and read.

"AND MY FINAL CONCLUSION WAS THAT IF THESE CHILDREN OF MINE WERE LIBERATED, THEY WOULD ALL DIE OF STARVATION OR WORSE. SOME

MIGHT LIVE FOR WEEKS—LIKE WILD ANIMALS LIVE IN THE WOODS—BUT EVENTUALLY THEY WOULD DIE. IT MAY BE THAT EVEN THE MOST INTELLIGENT OF OUR NATION WILL HAVE A HARD TIME TO SURVIVE, BUT THERE CAN BE NO FUTURE AND NO HOPE FOR THESE POOR THINGS I HAVE CARED FOR THESE LONG YEARS.

"AND SO I AM SENDING THEM HOME. IT IS A HAPPY THOUGHT TO ME THAT THESE CHILDREN HAVE A HOME TO GO TO AND A FATHER WHO IS MORE KIND AND WISE IN HIS DEALING WITH THEM THAN I HAVE BEEN ABLE TO BE. I AM SENDING THEM HOME! AND YET THESE CHILDREN LOVED ME AND TRUSTED ME. IN DOING THIS DEED I HAVE SHATTERED TRADITIONS OF A LIFETIME. I DID WHAT SEEMS BEST FOR THEM, BUT TO ME IT WAS A LOSS OF ALL THE BEST IN MY ETHICAL LIFE.

"I CAN ONLY COMPENSATE BY JOINING THEM IN A BETTER WORLD."

So Dr. Jones dropped ten drops of the medicine on his tongue, blew out the flickering candle, and went into the darkness to find his children. Two years later the message was found on his desk with all that remained of a brave man, still seated with his head in his arms.

CHAPTER TEN
The Right to Live

Winter was approaching. The Hubler family was prepared for it. They had received some help from Stafford, but even without that, they would have done fairly well. They were learning not only to live the life of pioneers, but also to accommodate themselves to the conditions of the new Stone Age.

Paul had made some traps and every day brought in some fresh meat or some skins. Ruth was learning to make articles of clothing out of the skins. Even Angelica in her play was preparing for the new life. Her dolls were growing up in a non-metallic period.

Every morning Paul would start out to make a round of his traps. Late afternoon found him back in the house. The entire family was comfortable. They had the necessities of life, though entirely deprived of the luxuries of their former home in New York. They often talked about that city. Now that Hubler was a little more sure of the future, he had more time to talk.

"I've often wondered just why men like Stafford did not send expeditions into the city," he said one evening. "There must be a lot of plunder there that would be useful for many years to come. Think of the full storehouses, the department stores, even the private homes, deserted like ours was. Some day when I have a chance I'm going to talk about it to him."

"I'm afraid that it's all rather mussed up," replied his wife. "You remember what happened to our canned goods; and then just as we left our apartment, the faucets started to leak. I believe that the city was flooded. Think of all the water pipes going to pieces. Perhaps by now many of the buildings have fallen down. It was really the steel that held them up toward the sky. I think that some day Mr. Stafford will go to the city, but it seems to me that his idea is to become absolutely independent of the past. Anything we took from the city would only last so long—and the time would come when we would have to learn how to make things or go without, so the sooner we begin, the better we'll be able to live on."

The next morning Hubler started, as usual, to make a round of his traps. A light snow had fallen during the night and the woods had turned into fairyland. He determined to make a larger circle than usual in the effort to locate some new hunting grounds up on the mountains. He was four miles from home when he saw smoke.

That was enough for him.

He had never seen smoke in that direction before.

And smoke meant human beings. He wanted to know what kind.

Born and raised in the city, he had behind him a long line of frontier ancestors. His forebears had fought the Indians so often that they had almost turned into Indians themselves. Once Paul Hubler set his feet on the bare ground, he had reverted to type. Call it inherited memory, or any other name, the fact remained that he had become a natural and very efficient woodsman.

So he started to find out where the smoke was coming from.

Two hours later he was motionless on an overhanging shelf of rock. Fifty feet below him was the fire and around that fire were fifty men, escaped from Sing Sing. They had raided a farm, killed a cow, and now were busily engaged in eating it and trying to keep warm around the fire.

There was no doubt about the fact that they were a menace to society. Paul could hear them talking in the jargon of the New York underworld. A lot of the slang he could not understand but he had no difficulty in catching the drift of their conversation. They were tired of living in the forest, and too lazy to build cabins. They had killed and robbed, but now there were no more isolated families, no easy plunder. The winter was going to be cold and long.

And they planned to attack the Stafford farm, kill the men, take possession of the buildings, and add the women to their gang. It was not an unusual plan. Similar collections of degenerates had been doing just that thing ever since the beginning of the Metal Doom. The unusual part of it was that they were talking rather loudly and Paul Hubler was on the overhanging rock.

He had heard enough, and left as silently as he had come. Once away from the vicinity he traveled as he had never traveled before. He came to the edge of the wood; he came to the house and found Ruth and Angelica safe, and then, without pausing to tell her the reason for his haste, he told her to put on her wraps and get ready to leave the house.

"We're going to see Stafford," he said. "I have to see him."

It was a long walk. They took turns carrying the little girl. The road had three inches of snow on it, pulling, dragging at their feet. At last they came to a well-built, wooden fence. A man was slowly walking up and down the crossroads. He walked up to Paul.

"You have to stop, and turn around," he said sharply. "This road is private."

"Better times are coming," answered Hubler.

The man smiled.

"In that case you can go on. Want to see the Boss? He's up at the house. You look tired. Supposed I carry the baby for you to the end of my beat, and then one of my buddies can help you out. You look tired."

"Not so much tired as worried," acknowledged Hubler.

Soon they were being hastily welcomed by Stafford.

"I thought you people had decided we were not good enough for you to associate with," he said with a laugh.

"It wasn't that, Mr. Stafford." Ruth replied seriously. "We wanted to make a real effort to get along for at least one winter on our own resources, and we could have done it, only Paul became frightened."

"I'm betting it was something serious, Mrs. Hubler. Your husband doesn't impress me as a man who would worry over trifles."

Paul then told his story. He told it in the greatest detail, not omitting any of the crimes the various members of the criminal gang had bragged about. He ended with the simple statement:

"I thought you ought to know about it as soon as possible."

"You were right. It looks like a very serious matter. I'm going to call my advisory group together. We've talked over such a possibility before, but so far it hasn't been a real emergency. I want whatever action we take to be the best thought of not one man, but of all the thinkers in our community."

So, within a short time, Paul Hubler was repeating the story to an earnest group of twenty men, each a specialist in his line of physical or mental endeavor. They listened intently. Then Stafford called on the oldest man of the group, a man who directed the agricultural life of the community. He was highly respected by his fellow workers. He began:

"When I was a young man I had a dog. He was a cross between a collie and a foxhound, and when he reached his growth he was fairly large. Now there were a lot of dogs in that section larger and heavier than my dog, but my dog never lost a fight. When he decided to fight another dog he simply walked up to him and jumped; there was no warning. The other dog was conquered before he realized there was a fight.

"I think we ought to act that way. These men by their own statements have been guilty of murder and worse. They're thinking of killing us, and taking our property. They even talk of taking our women. There is only one thing to do. Surround them and exterminate them."

"You would not capture them and give them a chance to leave this part of the country?" asked Stafford.

"Absolutely not. We might succeed, but we simply expose others to the same dangers we escape from. It wouldn't be friendly. We didn't ask for it, but this has become our problem. Let us settle it."

The old farmer sat down.

The vote taken proved that he had voiced the opinion of all present. Then Stafford said a few words:

"Ever since the beginning of the changes produced by the Metal Doom, I've been convinced that there had to be an elimination of the unfit. I hope that we'll always take care of our aged, but for the criminal I saw no hope. Our social order is too weak to imprison him and support him in idleness, and at the same time we cannot allow the psychopathic personalities to remain at liberty. They're too dangerous to the decent people in any community. I'm sure that at the present time there are lions and tigers in our woods escaped from the various Zoological Gardens of our land. If we found one of them, we would kill it. This band of criminals is a greater menace than as many wild animals. There is nothing to do except to protect ourselves. We'll leave here early in the evening. Hubler can guide us."

CHAPTER ELEVEN
The First Killing

It would be impossible in a short narrative to completely cover the entire history of this period of the Second Stone Age, or even to thoroughly describe the changes effected. Other historians, no doubt, would stress portions of the transition that this tale completely omits. What is attempted here is to give a general description of the change in civilization, and especially lay emphasis on the new attitude humanity assumed in dealing with problems of life.

For it's a well-recognized fact that the leaders in the new social order early realized that the old solutions of old problems could not be of further use to mankind. Everything had changed, and the change came so suddenly that it was fortunate there were many groups of men who were possessed of sufficient intelligence and imagination to see at once the necessity for the adoption of an entirely new code of social and ethical laws.

The events centering around the first killing showed the wisdom of their attitude toward the new laws of society. For centuries the legal profession had made a game out of the matter of law violation. Once a man was arrested for a crime, a game of legal chess started between two lawyers and the question was not so much an effort to establish the guilt or innocence of the prisoner as to determine which lawyer was the shrewdest. Certain phases became shibboleth, such as EVERY MAN IS INNOCENT TILL PROVEN GUILTY, and that NO MAN CAN TWICE BE PUT IN JEOPARDY OF LIFE OR LIMB FOR THE SAME OFFENCE.

The attitude of the legal profession was deeply appreciated by the criminal of the late electrical age. Irrespective of the blackness or number of his crimes, the arrested criminal asked for every possible consideration from the law, and his lawyers took advantage of every loophole in the law to prevent the administration of justice to the prisoner.

Obviously, all this elaborate legal machinery broke to pieces with the smashing of civilization. There being no jails, there could be no such thing as keeping an accused man behind the bars for several years while his trial was fatally procrastinated until even the ablest witnesses had forgotten what it was all about. There being no money, there could be no more bail, and even straw bonds were an impossibility, for there were no longer any courts.

The partial details of the first killing are given to show the necessity of the act and also to show that the criminal mind had failed to appreciate the change that had taken place in his treatment. Up to this time, the criminal's chief fear was in being arrested. Now a far greater menace faced him.

It was full moon that December night. Paul Hubler, walking silently through the snow, led a company of sixty silent men. They were armed with bows and arrows, spears and stone axes. All of them were expert archers, and had elm bows and yard-long arrows that would have aroused the envy of Robin Hood save for the fact that all the arrows were flint tipped. The snow was just deep enough and soft enough to deaden the footfalls. Talking had been forbidden.

They came finally to the forsaken home of the Hublers. From here on Paul had to show his woodsmanship. He felt sure that he knew the way for the next four miles. Daylight, the first dawn on the white snow, showed him that he was half a mile from the bandit camp. A thin column of smoke showed in the frosty air. There was a short consultation and then the sixty men split into three groups, each of which approached the smoke from different sides. Stafford and Hubler made for the overhanging shelf of rock where Hubler had first heard of the gangsters' plans.

The fire was blazing and the convicts were eating breakfast. They were talking about their plans for the day, the capture, plundering and burning of the Stafford properties. They said enough to convince Stafford of their guilt, even if he hadn't been fully satisfied before.

The weird cry of a hoot owl rang through the wood.

It was answered by other owls.

And then Stafford stood up on the overhanging rock.

"I want you men to listen to me," he said.

The convicts jumped to their feet. Every man seized his club. They were not afraid of one man but they were perplexed at seeing him there. At least they kept still.

"We have your record," continued Stafford. "We know what you have done before today and we know what you were going to do today. We tried you last night and sentenced you."

"Whacha mean?" asked one of the leaders, adding a few useless but very powerful obscenities.

Stafford simply put his hands to his mouth, hooted, and the killing began.

From the surrounding wood came the peculiar melody of twanging bowstrings and the swish of arrows cutting the air.

The convicts began to fall, clutching at the arrow shafts. Hubler and Stafford had left the rock to join their men.

The surviving criminals tried to find shelter but there was none. They tried to run, but that was useless, the arrows were swifter. At last only two men were standing against the rock. One was a murderer who had first been a lawyer.

Stafford told his men to take their spears and finish the killing. He led them. In fact he and Hubler walked up to the two unwounded men.

"You can't do a thing like this and get away with it," blustered the lawyer. Time had gone backward with him; once again he was in the electrical age, bluffing, twisting, squirming, making use of every legality to evade punishment. "Don't you know this is murder? If we're guilty, why not arrest us and give us a trial? You say we're criminals? Why, you have broken every law there ever was during the last ten minutes."

"Sure thing!" echoed the other man. "You can't do a thing like this. You'll pay for this. Just wait till I get a lawyer."

"We are going to kill you," said Stafford, quietly.

"You can't do it!" yelled the lawyer.

"Can't we?" asked the leader, plunging his spear in, just below the ribs.

Hubler made his kill without comment.

A man came up and touched Stafford on the shoulder.

"All the men are down, Boss, but some of them are just wounded."

"Finish them," was Stafford's whispered order.

"We'll leave them where they fell," he said to Hubler. "In years to come this place will be visited and those who come will feel that something happened here."

"Something *did* happen," replied Hubler. "This marks the beginning of a new justice."

Back the men of the community went. Back through the snow. White faced and cold and shivering they went back through the snow.

"I never killed a man before," said Stafford.

"I have," replied Hubler. "I killed a man once who was trying to hurt Ruth. I never did before, but I'm going to keep on killing anyone who tries to hurt Ruth or my baby."

"Are you sure it was right? Perhaps we should have given them a chance to fight?"

"They had the same chance to fight that they gave all their victims."

"But that man spoke about law?"

"Mr. Stafford. All the law that man knew is dead."

Back in the community the sixty men were welcomed by their women and children. There was rejoicing over the fact that none had been killed, none even injured. A special dinner was served, and some speeches made after dinner. Not a word was said about the affair of the early morning; it was not even hinted at.

The Hublers were assigned a comfortable bedroom. Angelica was put to bed under a Galloway fur lap robe, which she pretended changed her into a bear. She growled and tried to bite her father.

But at last she decided to change back into a little child.

"I love you, Angelica," said her father, "and I'm glad you're a little girl instead of a little boy."

"Thank you," said Angelica, and went to sleep.

Ruth and Paul sat before the fire. Ruth whispered:

"Do you know what the night is, Paul? This is Christmas Eve. Centuries ago, on this night, Christ was born in Bethlehem. He came to bring love and peace to the world."

The man shut his eyes. Once again he saw the look of astonishment on the face of the gangster as he felt the stone spear strike him. He looked around the room and seemed to see the dead, stretched on the ground, with here and there blotches of red on the snow.

He held Ruth closer, as he whispered back:

"I wish Christ had been born on some other day."

CHAPTER TWELVE
The First Christmas

During the night some of the women had decorated the main hall of the Stafford house. The Christmas program had long been provided for. There were to be gifts for all the little ones, toys and dolls carved out of wood and bone, and decorated with bits of lace and old dresses, sewed with bone needles.

All of the little community were to eat Christmas dinner together. There was no instrumental music, but all knew the old carols; and pleasure and happiness were welcomed guests. The women were happy, the children merry and the men—the men were just a little more serious than seemed to be appropriate.

The food was excellent, meat roasted over the flame, bread cooked in the brick oven, vegetables boiled in earthen pots, all served on china plates and eaten with wooden spoons. There was milk for the little children.

After the dinner there were speeches in plenty, with jokes and laughter. Life was different, but human nature was very much the same as it had been. Irrespective of changes, life had been kind to those who had sought and obtained the shelter of the Stafford colony.

There were a thousand unanswered questions, ten thousand unsolved problems, but for the minute these were forgotten in the effort to be happy—just for a minute.

And then the tide turned.

One of the sentries rushed in and whispered to Stafford. He beckoned a half dozen men with his eyes and walked out of the banquet hall. Out on the front gallery of the house they waited for him, two wild-eyed men leaning against the railing in their exhaustion.

"We've come to warn you," they both said. After that, one did the talking, the other falling to the floor and dying there from his wounds. "There is a mob of crooks sweeping this way. They're killing and burning everything in their path. They have horses, and they are fast. They heard of your place and swear to eat Christmas dinner here. They killed our wives and burnt our homes."

"How many?" asked Stafford.

"Over a hundred."

"Where from?"

"Up the Hudson."

"Good. Go in and eat. Sorry about your friend. Ring the alarm! Call all the men in."

"Fortunately most of them are here, Mr. Stafford," one of the sentinels replied.

"That's true. It's Christmas. Keep the women inside and we'll go out to do our talking. No use worrying them."

Seventy men were all there were in the colony. Stafford did not waste time. He called the names of twenty of them.

"You stay here in the house and guard the women," he ordered, "and the rest of you get your arms and horses ready. We ride to the North Fence. This affair is not going to be a slaughter, it's going to be a fight."

The only argument came from the twenty selected to remain. Paul Hubler was one of them.

"It's not right," he told Stafford. "I ought to go with you."

"You stay. It's all arranged. If anything happens to me you have to help save the colony."

The fifty men never went back to the house. There were no farewells said. They simply went to the stables, saddled their horses, arranged their weapons and rode away.

At every window faces pressed against the glass, women's faces and the faces of little children.

The fifty rode at a gallop to the North Fence. No time to spare. Doom was faster than the feet of horses. But when they came to the fence, no enemy was in sight.

Stafford called out the names of twenty of his best horsemen:

"Leave your bows and arrows here. Take all the horses up to the maple grove. Tie thirty and leave your spears there. Be ready to mount and charge when the time comes. If they break through, come anyway. The thirty of us will stay here and hold them. I don't want one of them to die on our land. We'll kill what we can but you have to mop up."

The place was well selected for a battle. The stone fence ran for several miles on both sides of the road. It was bull strong, stallion high and pig tight. It came up squarely on both sides of the road, and across the road there was a gate. But it was not part of Stafford's plan to close the gate. A closed gate was a warning, an open gate an invitation.

The day passed, and then the sun turned into a red ball of fire. The rouged sky looked angry and cold. Then the riders came into view, a motley, sordid group, laden with plunder and their souls charged with a hundred crimes. They were bad men, not brave, but men who would fight like rats if caught in a trap.

The North Fence looked like one more stone fence to them. They came on at a slow trot. Their horses had been badly cared for, poorly fed, and savagely ridden.

The leaders were almost through the gate when ten men sprang forward and plunged their lances with the fury of desperation into horses and men.

In a minute of time the passage was blocked with a mass of kicking horses and cursing men.

And the ten men kept on stabbing with their lances tipped with six inches of sharp flint, stabbing at everything that moved, drawing their lances back and replunging them. Not for nothing had daily practice been held at this use of the spear.

Simultaneously the remaining twenty archers stood up behind the fence and started to shoot. This was archery with a vengeance, not shooting at a mass, but each arrow deliberately aimed at a man. Not a sound from one side of the fence except the grunts of the lancers as they lunged forward and the twanging of the bows as the arrows sped.

Half of the horses were down.

And then the mounted men charged from the shelter of the maple trees. At the beating thunder of galloping hoofs the bandits still horsed, turned, and Stafford realizing that the fight at the best would be unequal, knowing that soon the arrows would be gone, cursed his stupidity in sending away the thirty horses.

But down along the outside of the fence they came, bridles tied together, two men leading them, and Stafford, with a cheer, ordered his men to mount.

Now the enemy was caught between the hammer and the anvil. They fought. They had to. Armed with clubs they did their best to save their lives and kill. But here were no isolated farmers, overwhelmed by numbers. Opposed to them were picked men on splendid horses, men who had for months been training in the use of the stone ax. Soon the fight had turned into a flight, and the flight into a deadly ending.

Stafford's men came back. That is most of them came back. Five were killed. During the next twenty-four hours three more died. Stafford sat on his panting horse as his men gathered around him. He looked at them, and then asked:

"Are they all dead?"

"We think so."

"Make sure. Kill the wounded horses; take your ropes and open the gate. We'll leave our injured men here under guard until we can send the carts for them. I thank you, my friends, for what you have done this day. I feel that it has taught us a lesson. The day for our splendid isolation is passed."

Later on a man rode up to him.

"Boss, the job is finished. We have no prisoners. But we want to take our dead back with us and the wounded men want to go back. They think they can stand the ride better than staying here and waiting for the carts to come for them."

"How are you going to take our dead?" Stafford replied.

"Please, sir, we thought we would take turns carrying them in our arms. The women would not like it, their women, if we left them here, even for a little while."

Stafford started to cry. Poor fellow! There was no woman waiting for him to come back, dead or alive; he hated to face the other women and tell them the news. He waved assent, spoke to his horse and started the trek toward home.

And the hundred motionless men laying scattered over the meadows, faces turned toward the growing moon, thought, if they thought at all, that life had played them a scurvy trick.

Once home, every attention was paid to the wounded. After all was done that could be done, the solitary physician took Hubler and Stafford to one side.

"Three of them are going to die," he whispered. "We might save them if we had the instruments, but they all disappeared with the rest of the metals and the stone makeshifts are not much use."

"It can't be helped," replied Stafford dully. "Tell their women as kindly as you can. Have you any morphine to give them? I don't want them to suffer."

"I have some. You know I asked you to organize an expedition to some city, to see if we could get some drugs, and surgical supplies."

"I know. My fault. I never realized that it might end in a fight to the death. I will—trust me—do the best I can. Right now, I must confer with my advisers and then sleep."

Six of them met in Stafford's office an hour later. Hubler was one of the six.

"Today's affair convinced me," said Stafford, "that we have underestimated the size of this job. In the space of twelve hours we met and destroyed about one hundred and fifty desperate bandits operating in two gangs. Their code of morals is entirely different from ours. Today we were successful. Tomorrow we may fail. We know nothing about what is going on in the world beyond us. We've lived a life of smug contentment, in a world of dreams. If a thousand men had come up to the stone fence they would be in this house now and we would be looking at the moon, like the men we killed. This place made a wonderful stock farm, but I feel it has its limitations as a place to defend against an army. I'm not discouraged but I'm anxious for the future. This morning we had seventy men. Tonight sixty-five, and the doctor says three more will die tomorrow. What is to be done?"

"Build a fort," replied Hubler. "And tell the world to come and take us. Stop being idealists and dreamers and develop an army of our own. Have other groups join us; and then we can defend ourselves."

CHAPTER THIRTEEN
Fort Telephone

They all went to bed that night rather exhausted from the unusual events of the previous twenty-four hours. The next morning the council of war was begun.

As a rather delicate compliment, Paul Hubler was called upon to open the discussion.

"Because he has imagination," explained Stafford.

"And that kept me most of the night," replied Hubler. "Seriously speaking, I was restless and when I did sleep, I dreamt rather horrible things. It was all because I was sure we were in for a bad time.

"We have learned something about it. Naturally we made some mistakes, but they can be corrected.

"The first thing we have to have is a fort. They largely went out of fashion during the World War, but now—without artillery and in an age of Stone—it seems they would be very useful. I never saw a fort, never helped to build one, but it seems we'll need a lot of timber and a lot of stone. Both stone and timber are going to be hard to get without metal tools, but there are a lot of old stone houses around here, and any number of telephone poles. Let us select a hill, and it has to have a living spring on it. Tear down some houses and build four or five towers with little windows in them. Run a ditch around the hill connecting the towers and in that ditch set up the telephone poles touching each other and tied together with ropes. Fill in the ditch, tamp it, and stiffen the poles in the rear with stone and dirt. Have platforms made for the archers.

"Inside the fort have little houses built for the various families. Build storehouses. Have enough fodder to keep cattle. Build reservoirs for water. Establish ammunition piles of stone and stores of arrows. Build catapults to throw large stones; train men to aim them and estimate distances.

"But that's just one fort. Try and have our neighbors build another one twenty miles away. Have beacons of wood on mountaintops ready to fire as danger signals. Find out who our allies are and how much we can depend on them. Consider every group of men our enemies until they prove that they are decent people. Learn to fight against overwhelming odds and keep on fighting.

"I believe that for a while all our effort should be spent in perfecting our defenses. The greatest luxury we can look for is safety for our women and children. On them depend the security of our future decades. Instead of spending time trying to build looms, and manufacture earthen pots, we should search the cities and bring back everything we need. Time enough twenty years from now to learn how to spin and weave—now we must spend our time in perfecting means of security.

"In the first Stone Age, prolonging of the life of the individual and securing the perpetuity of the race were the two great objects of life. In the second Stone Age we must not lose sight of this. Culture, ethics, past education, the fine arts, sciences, all must bow for the time to the securing of safety for the men who are worth while and breeding and rearing of worthwhile children.

"You ask me what I think? My answer is to start tomorrow and build a fort, and when that fort is built start filling it with necessities of life from the cities. It is going to be the work of months. When it's finished will be time enough to talk about the luxuries of life, the culture of the past."

"I think that some of us ought to go on with our special work," said a man who had been a writer of books. "For several months I've been writing a history of this period. I want to go on with it."

"What is the use of a history if there is no one left alive to read it?" countered Hubler.

At this point Stafford took the floor.

"I think Hubler has said all there is to say. We're barbarians living in a stone age and we might as well admit it. We know a lot more than the men of the first Stone Age but I'm not sure that our superior intellect makes us better able to cope with the problems that face us. But one thing is sure. We have to save the worthwhile people; the race has to go on. It may be conceit on my part, but I feel that we're better fitted to make the future race worthwhile than were the men we killed today. I think we ought to build this fort. We can have our architect draw plans for it and I think I know the very place to put it. We should all get to work. There is a little colony ten miles below us. I'll go down there and ask them to join us in building the fort. They can share it with us in time of danger. We'll build it along the lines Hubler suggested and we'll call the place Fort Telephone.

"I'm sold on the proposition. I don't want to force any of you to it, but you must see that it's the sensible thing to do. If any of you differ with us, you can leave the colony. It may be easier to wave a quill pen than to wrangle with a telephone pole, but in the long run the telephone poles will help us live longer.

"For this era is going to be long in stabilizing. It's going to be the survival of the fittest. It is a test of courage. We will build Fort Telephone."

CHAPTER FOURTEEN
Mackson Returns

ONCE the decision was made to build Fort Telephone, there was no delay. The entire resources of the Stafford Colony were directed toward the completion of that task. It was not a small one by any means.

Fortunately, the winter was a severe one. The snow remained thick on the ground until nearly the end of March. Stone boats were made and house after house was demolished and carted piecemeal to the site of the fort. Stone fences were torn down. Whenever possible, telephone poles were rooted out of the earth and snagged to their locations. When spring came much of the building material was in place ready to begin operations. At the best it was a heart-breaking task—digging ditches, moving stones, lifting the poles in place, tamping the dirt around them.

The men from the Mason Colony came to help and thus added thirty-five men to the working force. June found the place capable of standing an assault if not an actual siege. Part of the men were detailed for agriculture, the rest kept on working; at last the women stopped their housekeeping and helped carry stones and pull on the ropes. As the days went by, no new danger appeared—nothing happened. At times many of the men thought that nothing *would* happen, that it was all a weird nightmare and that the fort was a useless anachronism.

But at last it was finished. The little huts inside the enclosure were capable of housing a hundred families, three hundred people. There was a great deal to be done as far as the gathering of stores were concerned but the labor of building was at an end. Christmas day found a tired but contented band of people.

On Christmas day three bearded strangers rode up to the Stafford House. Mackson of Vermont and two of his guard.

Now it could be seen that they were not birds, but men in gliding machines. And from the gliders dropped death!

The others had died on the long trip across the country. It was a return from their great adventure.

Stafford realized the importance of whatever message Mackson had for them. He knew that it might be hopeful or hopeless. He did not want to discourage the rank and file of his followers and so, uncertain and cautious, he called in six of the leaders, Hubler, the man of imagination; Peterson, the architect; Johnson, the ranking officer of the new army; Van Rocklin, the scientist; Mason, of the Mason Colony; Wagner, the farmer and lastly himself. That made eight, with Mackson.

Mackson needed no introduction. He made no elaborate peroration; he simply placed on the table a paper.

"There it is, gentlemen. That is our new constitution. I've been gone sixteen months. I went to the Pacific by the Santa Fe Route and returned over the Lincoln Highway. Of course, there is a lot of the United States I never saw, but if the rest of it's like what I did see, I'm glad I didn't see it. I have the signatures of over two hundred communities like yours and like mine in Vermont. I suppose there are three hundred similar adventures going on in the old U.S.A. Every community I visited had the same ideas and the same ideal as we have. They were all glad to see me. They welcomed the idea of a new union. They were all composed of thinking, hard working idealists who had banded together for mutual help. If we could get the people of these colonies to all live in one state, we could do something. As it is they're scattered over too much territory."

"Do you mean to tell me," asked Stafford, "that in your opinion there are only about three hundred such colonies in all the United States, and each colony about like ours in size?"

"That's my estimate."

"But that's only about a hundred thousand people!"

"I suppose so."

"But—where are...? Why, man! That's impossible! Where are the people? We used to have a hundred and twenty-five million in the States. What—what happened to them?"

"It's a mess," answered Mackson.

"Go and tell us," urged Hubler, kindly. "I think I know; I think we all know. I've stayed awake at night trying to—well, trying to imagine what had happened. Go on and tell us."

"All right. Here goes. In the first place we saw most of the large cities. The main highways passed through most of them. The cities are gone, especially the business sections. You see the buildings were simply built around structural iron and when that rotted the buildings simply collapsed and the streets were not wide enough to hold the debris, so they just filled up, fifty to seventy-five feet, of every possible kind of wealth—just junk. In the residential sections it was a little better because the buildings were not so high and there was more wood used. I don't know how many people were killed in the city. Perhaps many millions left in time but there must have been as many millions who thought they would stick it out, and died in the first collapse.

"In the country things were a little better. The people were nearer the sources of food, the country people more accustomed to making use of their hands. If they were far enough away from the city, the country people didn't do so badly, for a while. But those who lived near the large cities were simply over-run. At first the urbanites were willing to pay money, but very soon their money gave out; the food was used up and then began a fight for life between the people in the country and the visitors from the cities. It was a fight for life. Every farmhouse was a little fort, every farm a battle ground. When the city people won, they wasted the food through ignorance. When the farmers won, they simply had to start fighting all over again. I talked to the heads of the various colonies who signed our constitution, and all they could tell me of those first months was that it was KILL, KILL, KILL! Or be killed. It didn't last long. The people from the city had no stamina, their women were weak, their children puny. They died like flies. The main highways are marked, not by signboards but by bodies and bones. Disease came, and at last winter. Only the strong survived, and they were only of two groups. One class is represented by the various colonies, the other class are escaped criminals and former gangsters."

"We know about that last kind," remarked Stafford.

"I suppose so. You can tell me about it later. Now for the sections. I didn't see much of it but they tell me that the white population in the real Southern States is wiped out. For generations they held the Negro down with firearms. When it came to the point where clubs and stones were the only weapon, the Negro rose and that was the end of white supremacy. Of course the colored man has his own problems of survival now south of the Mason and Dixon Line.

"West of the Mississippi it's different. Texas, New Mexico and Arizona are fighting for their lives against the waves of Mexicans and Indians from over the border. They're having real war down there. Every Texan I met said the Lone Star was going to keep on shining. They're even talking about forming an army and going down to Mexico and settling the thing once and for all. They were interested in our proposition but so busy with their own troubles that they didn't have much time to give it. They signed on the dotted line, but I'm not sure how much it will mean.

"California is very much like New York. They still have a lot of climate but had to admit that the tourist business was at a standstill. They're trying to form a republic west of the Rockies and wanted to be friendly with us, but at the same time they felt rather isolated. You would understand how they feel after you have made the journey out there on horseback."

"So you think the criminal element is a real menace?" asked Hubler.

"I do. Everywhere we went the serious thinkers were worried about it. You see the escaped criminal and the gangster were used to fighting for what they thought belonged to them. They were used to killing, to running in herds and packs and gangs. It was just second nature to them. The complete overthrow of all the organized restraint gave them an unusual sense of freedom. For the first time the policeman was not standing on the corner. They have all organized. In some districts their bands number hundreds. Of course they fight among themselves but mainly they're killing the decent isolated country people."

"How about the change in the country, the fields and the animals?" asked farmer Wagner.

"There are a lot of wild dogs. They're gathering in packs. Out west the lions are growing in numbers and courage. We heard a lot about escapes from the Zoological Gardens. I talked to one man who said he believed there were over two hundred lions and tigers in the United States. We saw a herd of elephants, and a lot of other wild animals escaped from various circuses. Of course most of them are shy, but in time the flesh eaters will start killing.

"As far as the land is concerned, it's going back to nature."

"Looks rather hopeless," commented Van Rocklin, the scientist.

CHAPTER FIFTEEN
Stafford Goes Away

The tired man from Vermont was put to bed. The leaders talked for a while longer and then all left except Stafford and Hubler. Paul had been asked to stay.

"It looks as though civilization had a grand smash, Paul," said Stafford. "Must have been rotten at the core to go to pieces so quickly."

"Something was wrong," agreed Hubler. "Looks as though the individual became too highly specialized, learned to do one thing and became incapable of doing anything else. Can't live that way in the Stone Age. A man has to be Jack-of-all-trades to survive."

"Of course the cities were doomed."

"Certainly; but if it hadn't been the Metal Doom, it would have been something else. Conditions were becoming too congested, too artificial; things had to break; something, somehow—what I want to say is that in some way the city, as a place of abode, was on the way to destruction anyway."

"Have you ever wanted to go back and see what happened to it, Hubler?"

"Sometimes. But that's just curiosity. I don't think I was ever really happy there; and I was born there. I'd like to go back and live in the old farmhouse where Ruth and I were when you first met us. That was a sweet place to live."

"Let me ask you a question. How would you like to take charge of this place? Be the leader of Fort Telephone?"

Hubler laughed as he replied. "What for? With you here? All the boys like you."

"I think I'm going away."

"What for?"

"I don't know. Just going. I guess I'm fed up on the life here. It's different with you. You have the wife and little girl. I'm just an old bachelor. We have the fort built now, and all you have to do is to fill the storehouses with supplies, and keep things going. I'm going to take my favorite horse, and I'm going to go out into the world and see what it looks like. Two years now and I haven't been more than five miles away from the house."

"Ask Mackson to be the head."

"No. He's popular with his men but he's not the right man for the commander of the Fort if anything happens. He couldn't anticipate trouble. Now you have imagination."

"You've said that before. Well, I won't argue with you. When are you leaving?"

"At daybreak. You tell the boys and say goodbye to Mackson. Tell them that if things get too hot up in Vermont then he and his company will always be welcomed here."

Hubler looked at Stafford anxiously.

"You'll take care of yourself and come back safe?"

"Sure. Don't you worry about that. Comes spring and I'll be here to look after the young stock."

"Take some of the men with you, won't you?"

"No. I want to have a good time. I don't want to bother with any men."

Back to his bedroom, Paul woke Ruth to tell her the news.

"Stafford is leaving the colony."

"I expected it."

"Why? Did he say anything to you?"

"No. But he's been restless. He's finished the fort and there isn't anything big here to do, so he's restless."

"I bet he has something up his sleeve."

"I suppose so. Stop talking so loud. You'll wake the baby."

At daybreak Stafford had an early breakfast, walked over to the stables, saddled his favorite horse, carefully tied on a stone tipped lance, a battle ax, a small tomahawk, his bow and arrow, and then with a warm handshake for all the stable men, rode off into the early sunrise.

There was a little snow on the ground, and the air was just cold enough to stimulate. The horse felt good, the rider felt good; everything seemed all right.

"I'm free from care," Stafford acknowledged. "For an old bachelor I was growing much too large a family. It was nerve racking; so now the family can shift for themselves as best they can while I go off adventure hunting. Let's see…shall it be the city or the wilder country? East or West? North or South?" He stopped briefly and surveyed the countryside. "I know what I'll do—the Mason colony has a flat boat; I'll have them take me across the Hudson, and then I'll go down the Delaware River Valley to the Water Gap. That was a favorite drive of mine in the good old automobile days. I always thought that Mount Minsi would be a fine place to build a fort. There are a lot of good cement roads over there and I guess if we go slow and are careful, the old horse won't go lame. I may locate a few new colonies down that way."

He spent the first night at the Mason Colony. As part owners of Fort Telephone they knew and respected Stafford. But they advised him not to cross the river.

"There's a lot of wild country over there and it's growing wilder all the time. Not many people, but lots of dog—and we hear some real lions."

"I always wanted to kill a lion," said Stafford.

Not being able to change his mind, they took him across the river. A week later he had circled around Port Jervis. Two days later he was at Milford. From there down to Bushkill, Shawnee and the Water Gap was a short ride.

The trip had been singularly devoid of excitement. The country was peculiarly depopulated. There were any number of stone houses, and he was always able to make himself fairly comfortable at night. In most of the barns there was hay for his horse, but the country people had all left. At Milford he found a partial explanation. There was a fort. Singularly it was very much like Fort Telephone, and around that fort over two hundred families were spending the winter. He had a long talk with the leader and made arrangements for mutual help in time of need.

They advised him not to try to go further south.

"It's a long trip to Easton," they said, "and there is nothing to see. There is another colony and fort in Cherry Valley but the Stroudsburgs are empty."

"Anybody living at the Gap?"

"Don't think so."

"I'm going anyway."

One of the older men took him to one side and whispered. "Don't want to scare you, but there are some tigers and lions down that way."

"You don't say so? Real ones?" The old man shook his head in assent.

"There's been some slaughter of livestock, any number of horses and cows killed by them."

Although the man's statement was issued as a warning, it was merely one more compelling reason for Stafford to go on. He planned it all out as he road along. If he could, he would utilize his bow and arrow; or—if the horse would stand for it—he would try top lasso the brute. If his mount was simply to frightened by the beast, he would tie the horse to a tree and go on foot, using his lance for the kill. He still had left the battle-ax, tomahawk, and his sharp flint-hunting knife.

"Have to be careful not to spoil the hide," he said to himself, with a grin.

At Shawnee he took a lengthy detour leading up the side of the mountain. It was a dirt road but it was in nice condition. He was partly influenced by the sight of smoke curling up through the frosty air. People had a fire there and he wanted to meet them. At the top of the road he suddenly saw what he was looking for.

Not a house, nor people—but a tiger.

It was in the middle of a little meadow surrounded on three sides by the forest and on the south side by the road. The tiger was leisurely eating his kill, a dead calf. If he saw Stafford and his nervous horse he paid no attention to them but kept on eating. The horse trembled and tried to turn around. Stafford tied him to a tree, slung his quiver of arrows on his back, took a lance and the bow and an ax in his hand and jumped over the fence. He was only about fifty yards away from the tiger. His striped tawny hide made a beautiful mark against the snow that lay across the meadow. Stafford took his heaviest hunting arrow, carefully estimated the distance between him and the tiger, then let it fly. It struck the beast's neck, back of the ear and passed completely through.

The tiger cried and charged. Stafford had time for one more arrow and then seized his lance. Fifteen feet from him the tiger jumped. In the air he was impaled on the stone point of the lance. It broke under his weight, but he was dead when he touched the ground. Stafford wiped his forehead. He was surprised to find that he was sweating freely. A woman came running out of the forest and across the meadow.

"You have killed my tiger," she cried, angrily.

CHAPTER SIXTEEN
A Lady and a Tiger

Stafford looked at the dead tiger and then at the angry woman. He never said a word in reply. She came closer, and he saw that her right hand held a small stone hammer, held by the handle and ready to throw. She repeated her accusation.

"You have killed my tiger!"

"Your tiger?" he asked in astonishment.

"Certainly! And what business have you anyway up here? Trespassing on our land and killing our pets. I have half a mind to kill you, you big brute, to go and kill a poor tiger who never hurt anybody."

"But it was eating that calf, Madam."

"It had to eat something, and anyway, it was our calf, and none of your business. What are you going to do about it?"

Stafford took out his hunting knife.

"I'm going to skin it for you," he said. "Seems strange to me, what you say, but if it *was* your tiger—and I don't for the life of me see what you were *doing* with a tiger—but if it was your tiger, it's a *dead* tiger now and the only good you could have out of it is the skin. So I'll skin it for you and take it to your house…if you'll let me."

"What did you kill it for?"

"Wanted to. Always wanted to kill a lion or a tiger. Heard there were wild ones down here, and thought I might have a chance."

Skinning a tiger under the best of conditions is not a small job and it's a larger one when a flint knife was the only knife available. The woman sat on a large stone and silently watched the process. At last Stafford finished, brought his lasso and tied the skin in a compact bundle. Then he fastened the other end to the horn of his saddle.

"Now if you tell me where you live, Madam," he said, "I'll drag this skin to your front door and drop it there. I guess you know how to peg it out and salt it."

"Don't call me Madam! Call me Doctor."

"You mean that you're a physician?"

"Certainly. Don't I look like a physician?"

"No. Most of the women physicians I've seen look a little old and worn out, while you look—well, just a little young."

"Perhaps that's because I haven't been working since the crash came. Since you have killed my tiger, I might as well let you bring the skin home. It's not far to the house, so I'll walk on ahead of you."

"I'll walk with you, Doctor, if you're willing."

Fifteen minutes later they came to an old brick schoolhouse. Two other women were standing at the door.

"Where have you been, Dotty?" asked one of them.

"Out feeding my tiger—and this man went and killed it, so I invited him back for dinner. This afternoon he's going to show me how to start tanning the skin."

"Hmmmm. Well, why not introduce everybody?"

"My name is Stafford," said the man nodding toward the women.

"And I am Doctor Perno, and these ladies are Doctor Brown and Doctor Hoffard."

"Pleased to meet you, ladies. Seems to be a lot of Doctors here."

"Yes. You see we lived here in the summer, so when the change came we thought it best to stay here. There are about ten other women around here. Quite a little colony."

"And no men?"

"Of course not. What would we want men for?"

"I see. I thought a man might be handy now and then, but evidently one is not needed here. So now I'll say goodbye and be on my way."

"We turned the garage into a barn," answered Dr. Perno, and you'll find room for your horse there and hay for him, and I guess the girls have something to eat and so you had better stay and show me about that skin."

In a short time the three Doctors and Stafford were seated at the table. Stafford looked around.

"You ladies seem to be real comfortable here."

"Yes," replied Doctor Brown, "and we were doing well...two cows and a few goats—and then the tiger came. Now there's nothing left. It took our last calf last night."

"And Dotty was so mad she took her tomahawk and said she was going to find that tiger and settle with him," added Dr. Hoffard.

Stafford looked quizzically at Dr. Perno, then said, "Yes, Dr. Brown. The business of having tigers for pets is a costly one at times. This one cost me my best lance. Perhaps it was a good thing for the tiger that I came along when I did. If Dr. Perno had found that cat first she would have been right brutal to it. As it was, all she was brutal to was the insolent stranger who killed her poor pet."

"Have some more beans," said the Doctor in question.

"And you ladies have lived here all these months and not had any trouble?" asked Stafford.

"The sun did not always shine," whispered Dr. Brown.

"We've had our ups and downs," added Dr. Hoffard.

"And now and then have our pets killed," purred Dr. Perno.

"And there are thirteen of you. All physicians?"

"Of course not. School teachers, and nurses, and even a retired lawyer."

"Well, well! Thirteen. That's an unlucky number. I feel that something is going to happen to one of you."

"Oh! Yes!" replied Dr. Perno. "Like having our tiger killed?"

"Something like that," laughed the man. "But seriously, ladies, you ought to have protection."

"Nonsense! No one ever comes here."

And at that the door was flung open and in rushed a number of women. There were excited questions and answers.

Everybody talked at once. Finally the story came out. The lookout (for it seems that the women really took turns watching from a high hill) had seen a small group of men on horseback come up the road. Before she could give warning, the first house of the feminine colony had been captured, the two women living there killed, and the house set afire.

"It's the old story," said Stafford, quietly. "You were just lucky not to have it happen before. Now you women stay here and shut the windows and doors and keep quiet. If the men come, you fight. I'm going to leave you."

Dr. Perno went up to him and put her hand on his shoulder.

"Where are you going?" she asked.

"Going to kill some more tigers," he said smiling.

"I'm going with you," she replied.

He shook his head.

"Not this time," he whispered. "This business of vermin hunting is not a nice one for ladies to engage in."

"You *will* come back?"

"Sure."

CHAPTER SEVENTEEN
Stafford Comes Back

Stafford looked a little old as he walked out to the garage and saddled his horse; things had taken a rather unexpected turn.

He knew that he had to go and kill those men. He felt fairly confident he could do so. He did not feel that he was a hero; he did not even feel afraid; just rather irritated at having to do something like that just at this particular time.

At a walk he rode the horse down the road. Soon he heard shouts and talking. He turned into the woods and hid behind a large rock. Ten men passed him, and their talk betrayed them. They were hunting women and the two they had met were too old. Stafford arranged his quiver so the arrows were easily grasped, and had his horse walk out on the road. He was now about seventy feet in back of his prey.

He stopped his horse and after careful aim sped an arrow. Almost before it had reached its mark another was in the air, and another. Three men tumbled to the ground. The other seven turned their horses, saw only one man and charged. Two more dropped and then Stafford charged to meet them, lance at point. He ran through a man, dodged the blows of the others and galloped up the road. Sixty yards up he turned his horse and again started to shoot. Two men were left and they charged. At least they were not cowards. One had his skull crushed, the other, as he galloped by struck Stafford's left arm and broke the bone. Stafford, holding his ax in his right hand and guiding his horse with his knees, pursued him. They met in front of the old school house. The bandit was armed with a club, and they fought it out, with the women watching from the windows. Stafford could not guard his left side and there the club fell crushing him to the ground. The bandit jumped off his horse, ran over to where Stafford lay, senseless on the snow, and raising his club, prepared to give the deathblow. The club dropped from his hands, he looked puzzled, and slowly sunk to the ground, his skull almost cut in half.

Stafford kept on sleeping. At last he woke. He looked around him. Everything looked strange. He was puzzled, could not remember what had happened. He shut his eyes. Again he opened them. A woman was sitting by his bed. He remembered now; at least a part of it.

"I had a dream," he said. "I thought I was home. "

"You are, dear," said the woman, kissing him.

"So that's the way of it," he said rather contentedly. "Just what happened? The last I remembered I was in a bad way. I think I must have made a failure of my last kill."

Dr. Brown came in just in time to hear that question and she answered it.

"It was like this. Dotty had a ringside seat, and when the umpire started to count you out she became restless and got into the fight. In other words, she killed another tiger."

"So that's the way it was?" said Stafford, looking at the woman. She started to blush.

"It wasn't anything. You killed a tiger for me, I killed one for you," she said.

"I see. Did you get the horses?"

"Yes. We have all ten in the pasture, and three of the men in the hospital."

"You mean you didn't... I mean you're taking care of them?"

"Certainly," answered Dr. Brown.

"They were rather badly hurt, but it was wonderful surgery. You killed the other seven, you and Dottie. What's the matter? You look as though you weren't pleased."

"Up our way," said Stafford, "we don't take prisoners."

"You don't mean that you kill them?"

"I think you heard me the first time, Dr. Brown."

The Doctor was puzzled. She went and talked it over with the other physicians. They came en masse and asked Stafford to explain his statement to them. He seemed tired and talked slowly, as though he were explaining simple facts to a group of children.

"I don't believe you women understand just what has happened in the world. You came up here, and it was a rather isolated and sheltered position and you were not where you could see the changes that took place in the social and judicial thinking of society.

"Life used to be considered a very wonderful thing, and everything was done to prolong life. It did not make any difference whether the life was of any value or not or whether the person deserved to live. The idiot, the epileptic, the insane, the degenerate and the criminal were all taken care of. In time of war prisoners were taken, and, even though they were not very well taken care of, at least their lives were spared. And it was only occasionally that a man was so bad that he was punished for his crimes by the taking of his life; in a large majority of crimes the criminal was simply imprisoned and the good people of the state were made to support him.

"It's all different now. The few groups of decent people who have managed to exist so far have all they can do just to keep going. All their energies have to be spent in self-preservation. The hopelessly insane, the uneducateable idiot, the hardened criminal have no possible place in the best communities of the new Stone Age.

"I'm the leader of a colony of about two hundred persons. We are trying to the best of our ability to survive. But that undertaking means that we can raise only normal children. We can't care for hopelessly insane, and under no circumstances can we—after a battle—expend our energy and provisions in the care of prisoners, wounded or not."

"Let me ask you a question," said Dr. Brown. "You are attacked by a band of escaped convicts. You win the fight. Many of your enemy are badly wounded. Do you mean to say that you kill them?"

"Yes."

"And if you had a little feeble minded child born in the colony, you would kill it?"

"Fortunately that hasn't happened yet, but the colony wouldn't agree to care for that child and allow it to become a member of the colony."

The lawyer of the group interrupted, "You have thrown away one of the greatest ethical possessions of humanity, the care of the unfortunate by the more fortunate, the most wonderful lesson of Christianity to mankind."

Stafford looked a little more tired as he replied:

"We haven't thrown away anything, Madam. But certain conditions were forced on us by the Metal Doom, and we've only done what we have had to do."

"You're terribly brutal," the lawyer replied. "I'm certainly glad you're not my husband. I wouldn't marry you if you were the last man on the earth."

"I'm sure of that, Joan," said Dr. Perno.

Four weeks later Stafford headed a little band northward from Shawnee. Through the Delaware River Valley they went northward, reversing the journey he had made when he went tiger hunting. At last they came to the Stafford Colony and Fort Telephone.

That night he held a meeting of the associate leaders of the colony. One of the men questioned the wisdom of his step.

"Looks rather foolish to me, Stafford. Might be all right to bring one woman here. We would have given you three rousing cheers, but when we saw you coming up the road, followed by thirteen women, we weren't sure that you had remained completely sane. What in the world can we do with thirteen women?"

"It was this way, boys," the leader replied. "These thirteen women were all highly educated, and between them just the finest lot of the old maids you ever met, and not so old either. I happened to find them and just in time. If I had come a day or so later, they would have all been killed. I became acquainted with them and I thought they would be of great help to our colony. You see, a lot of our boys are not married, nice enough boys, but never married when they could and then—when the crash came—it was too late. So, I thought it would be a good thing to bring back some wives for them—and I did."

"But those women won't marry our boys. They're Doctors and lawyers and teachers. They won't marry our cowboys and stable men."

"Won't they? Just wait and see. It's my opinion that every one of them will be married in a month or two. They probably never married before because men were too common, but now—it's different."

"Let me ask you a question, Stafford," said Hubler. "Are you going to marry one of them?"

"Never thought of that," said Stafford with a laugh. "I've been so busy bringing these women through danger that I never really thought of marrying one of them. Now you met them all at supper, Paul. Which one do you think I ought to wed?"

"That lawyer would be the best one."

"Okay with me," said Stafford.

CHAPTER EIGHTEEN
The Eastern Migration

The next day Stafford made an inspection of the Colony with Paul Hubler. He personally saw and spoke to all the people who lived within the shadow and protection of Fort Telephone. He saw all his favorite horses and all the newborn calves and colts. Everything was quiet and peaceful.

"Not a cloud in the sky," he commented to Hubler. "It all looks very much like the old days. Not as busy and noisy as it was then, but on the surface things are very much as they used to be. At times I think that I was over excited when I allowed you to persuade me into building Fort Telephone. I don't believe we shall ever need it."

"At least I've gone ahead with the storing of necessaries in it," replied Hubler. "All the time you were gone we filled the houses with grain and every possible thing we could need in case of a siege. I had the men make two trips to New York City, and while the plundering of that place is very difficult, we brought back a lot of stuff. You'd be surprised to see our card index. And we have all the huts whitewashed and furnished. If we had to, we could put four hundred people inside the fort, shut the gates and start providing for them, and I think we'd have provisions for several months."

"I'm not sure that we'll ever have to use the place, Paul. I've praised your imagination, but at times I've felt you had a little too much. Now, in regard to your idea of marrying that lawyer; that was just imagination run riot."

"Have you asked her to marry you?"

"No. Didn't have to. She told me that if I were the last man—"

He never finished the sentence. A horseman galloped up.

"You men are wanted at the house right away."

"Anything wrong?"

"Must be. A stranger was brought in by the sentinel, and then they came running down to the barn and told me to get the Boss back as soon as I could. Had a hard time finding you."

Later on the two men walked into the office of the Colony. A stranger stood up as they entered and introduced himself.

"I'm Webster, from Maine," he said simply. "Things are going wrong up there and they sent me down to give you a warning."

"Sit down and rest," urged Stafford. "You look tired."

"I am. Been riding hard."

"So, things are bad up in Maine?"

"Worse than bad. They just about wiped us out. We had five rather flourishing groups up there, doing fine, and then they came."

"Who are they?" asked Hubler.

"The Tartars."

"Not from Asia?" asked the astonished Stafford.

"I guess so. Of course, I never was over there and we can't talk their language, and even if we could, we've been fighting so hard that there was no time for conversation, but they look like the description in the histories, and they act like real Huns of some kind."

"Where did they come from?" queried Hubler.

"Must have come from Europe. First we knew they were in Maine. We had a colony of fishermen right on the coast and those of the colony who escaped said they just woke up one morning and there they were, in what seemed like hundreds of sailing vessels. They just landed—and that was the end of that colony and then they spread. We had a little warning and we started to fight, but it was a hopeless battle from the first. They nearly wiped that first colony out; only a few escaped. After that they just spread out and mopped up the entire state of Maine."

"Couldn't you do anything? Didn't you have arrows and spears, and stone clubs? Did you know how to fight?" asked Stafford.

"Of course. We had made weapons, and practiced in their use, but we were like children against those men. They had done nothing but fight with hand weapons for centuries and they were as much at home on horses as they would be on a chair. Besides, every fight was an unequal one. A colony or group of about one hundred fighting men against several thousand Asiatics. It was just slaughter after slaughter. No prisoners, no hope."

"And they're coming this way?"

"Looks like it. I've tried to spread the news. Another courier went up toward Vermont and Canada. We thought that we might make a united stand on this side of the Hudson. The battle will have to be fought in the open and to the death. When we're through, either we'll control the East or they will. If they win, it will mean more boats and more Tartars, and soon the entire western continent will be Asiatic."

"Have you any idea as to how many men we'll have in that army?"

"Not exactly."

"You're not even sure that the colonies will realize the danger and respond?"

"No. But we heard rumors that a number of them had signed some kind of a compact to assist against a mutual enemy."

"They did. A Vermonter took the paper to the Pacific Coast and back again; but only a limited number of those colonies could possibly respond in time to help stop the enemy east of the Hudson. Where do you think we ought to form a line?"

"Right here. On my way I passed that fence; your men called it the North Fence. I've seen some stone fences, but that's the best I've ever seen. If we had rifles, we could hold that fence against the world. That's where we ought to stand. I think we can form a force of a thousand men at least."

"And you think the battle ought to be in the open?"

"Yes. If we go into a fort, they'll simply flow around the place, leave enough force to hold it, and go on. Eventually, the people inside the fort would be starved out."

"A hand to hand battle," mused Stafford, "is not at all pleasant. We'll lose a lot of men."

"And if you don't have that kind of a battle, you'll lose them all."

"What do you think, Hubler?" asked Stafford.

"Something like this. Suppose we have a thousand Americans on one side of a stone wall and two thousand Tartars on the other side. Each army is equipped with the same kind of weapons—arrows, spears, clubs. But the Tartars are doing something they're used to; they've been fighting for centuries. We're just relearning arts of warfare that have been obsolete in our civilization for hundreds of years. Result? Not a chance in the world for the cultured American. We're brave, but those Tartars are going to win easily.

"Now...what do we have that the Tartars lack? Science of the highest form. When the crash came, we felt there was nothing we could not do in the field of science. Compared with our learning, the Tartars were idiotic children. In *some* way we have to make use of that scientific intelligence."

"But how can we," asked Webster, "when we have no metals?"

"That's the point. We have to apply our education in some way we never thought of before. The intelligence we used to have is still there; our inventors are still alive; we still have our scientists. This has to be a battle between intelligence and muscle, and always in the past intelligence has won. That's why man is ruler of the world today, even in a second Stone Age. That's why the most intelligent races have always been able to wipe out those of lesser intelligence."

"And what is your plan of battle?" asked Stafford.

"A rather simple one and rather impossible, it may be. I'd put a front line of defense at the North Fence. The women and children I'd put in Telephone Fort and there I'd put the married men. From this hour on I'd say to our scientists, 'Work! Think! Invent!' 'ON YOUR INTELLIGENCE DEPENDS THE SAFETY OF OUR PEOPLE!' Then I'd hold the North Fence as long as possible and when the time comes, I'd retreat to the second line of defense. When that's taken, those who are alive can go into the Fort. I hope, in the meantime, the scientists will solve the problem."

"Suits me," said Webster. "I'm going to bed. Mr. Stafford, will you send men into the neighboring country and tell them of the danger and ask them for help? Eastern Pennsylvania, New Jersey and New York should do something. I expect a thousand refugees from the New England States to come in during the next few days, but of course, many of that thousand will be women and children and tired and wounded men."

"Not all of them," said a new voice.

"Mackson!" simultaneously cried Stafford and Hubler.

"And a hundred Green Mountain boys with me!" laughed Mackson.

CHAPTER NINETEEN
Flight of a Tartar Tribe

It was not until some years later, after communication with Europe had been re-established, that the people of America gained a full understanding of the Asiatic menace that threatened to wipe out the little colonies of the Eastern United States.

For centuries the desert lands of Asia had bred broods of nomads. Tramps of the desert, they knew nothing except war, cared for nothing except their horses, weapons, and the open sky, and feared nothing except the silent enemy, Hunger. For a hundred years or more they would have food for all, horses, warriors, and even for the women and children. Their tents covered the plains like stars in the sky, their herds, uncounted and almost uncared for, provided all their needs. Then would come a year of famine, and, like caribou migrating, the Tartars would move, sometimes one way and at other times another way. Down into China, over the Himalayas to rich India, westward to Constantinople, even to Vienna. Northwest to Poland. Where they went they conquered, and boasted that where their horses tramped, the grass never again grew green. Rapine and plunder and slaughter. Pyramids of heads! Little valleys filled with bodies of the slain. And in a land of plenty they would stay, to become the nobility of an effete Russia, the Overlords of Paranoia, the land that made the Great War possible.

The Metal Doom had nothing to do with the latest of these migrations. It would have come anyway. But because of the onset of the second Age of Stone, the irresistible force met nothing to stop it. No immovable body in the form of Charles Martel stood in the way. European civilization had learned to fight with the weapons of scientific invention. When these arms were taken from them, the European went down in defeat. At last the Tartars stood on the eastern shore of the Atlantic Ocean.

This was simply one of periodic migrations. It was as instinctive as that of the lemmings in Norway, the swallows of Europe or the flight of the wild goose to Labrador. Back of it was no distinctive purpose, no cool, intelligent calculation, no purpose born of adult reactions to definite stimulae.

Instead, it was a slow, steady surging westward, constantly crashing its crushing criminal course, regardless of all opposition. And at last they reached the shores of the Atlantic.

For centuries the Dutch, Belgians, and Britons had sailed the sea. In boats of willow and skin, of wood propelled by oar and sail, in ships of iron with steam kettles in their darksome depths, they had sailed the sea. They had to go down to the water in ships or die of land sickness. When the Metal Doom came they sighed a day for their pretty playthings and then started to make other boats of wood, pinned together with wooden pins, and fitted with sails, primitive but beautiful.

The Tartars knew nothing of the sea. Their oceans of sand knew no other ship of the desert than the camel and the horse. They were nomads but not navigators. But they had to go West and west they went, in boats sailed by Europeans; and some ships sank and others were thrown back on the Irish coast; but enough came to the coast of Maine to allow a Tartar invasion of a continent hitherto immune from their ravages.

In Maine they first killed and then hunted for horses. Once on horses, they were at home; it was easier to kill on horseback. They went west and south and where they met other peoples they killed, for no other reason than the sheer joy of killing. Here and there they made pyramids of heads, not large pyramids, but of the correct shape and materials; and none of the Americans in their pathway were able to do anything but fight and die.

Down through Maine and Massachusetts they surged. And at last through Connecticut and towards the Hudson. Time meant nothing to them; geography was an empty term. All they thought of was to go on and on, and in the going kill.

They did not reach New York as quickly as Webster thought they would. He had traveled alone on the wings of despair, while they had come on in a group of two thousand, their hands and feet heavy with blood and satiated with killing. Thus, it was two weeks to a day from the time that Webster broke the news to the Stafford colony that the first riders from Tartary came within sight of the North Fence.

It was a peculiarly situated fence. Built of stone, it marked the northern boundary of the Stafford acreage. One end of it paused abruptly on a palisade that dropped three hundred feet into the Hudson. The other end ran into a primitive woodland, where the trees were so large and so close together that only a man on foot could pass through it. This wood was a mile wide and rested against a sheer mountain. There were two main roads. One passed through the North Fence and the other passed on the far side of the mountain.

On both sides of the stone fence ran as pretty a meadow as God ever greened for the pleasurance of his creatures. From the far side of the fence this meadow flowed downward until it came, a half mile away, to a little stream. Between this stream and the North Fence the Tatar tribe came to a definite pause in the fight. There was something in the appearance of that fence that made them feel it best to consider it carefully. Up to this time they had simply flowed over opposition. Now they stopped.

CHAPTER TWENTY
An Important Two Weeks

The day following Webster's arrival was a busy one for the Americans located at or near Fort Telephone. It was so busy that Angelica Hubler was not sure that she had a Father and Ruth Hubler was satisfied that her husband thought more of his position in the Stafford Colony than of his place as a husband and a father. It was not until twilight that he had a chance to see his little family. They walked out in the pasture after supper. It was a pretty clear evening. They walked quite a little way, so far that they were alone in the pasture. Paul talked to his wife about the problem everyone was trying to solve.

"The only chance we have to beat these people," he explained, "is to use our intelligence in some way so we can crush them. If we depend on our muscles, we're sunk."

"You ought to be able to do something," replied Ruth. "I thought that some of our best known scientists would be with us in a little while, when the other Colonies join us."

"They have the brains all right, and if it were in the old days, before we went into the age of stone, we'd have no trouble at all, but when we lost our metals, we lost everything."

Angelica felt very much out of it all. She tugged at her Father's hand:

"Daddy, what are those birds up there in the sky?"

"I think they're hawks, Little One."

"What are they doing, Daddy?"

"Looking around for something to eat."

"Are they flying, Daddy?"

"No, they're soaring."

And he explained to the little girl how the birds balanced themselves on their wings and, taking advantage of the currents of air, sailed back and forth without very much muscular effort. She listened gravely and then commented, "I wish I could do like that."

Hubler looked at her and then he shut his eyes. For a second, time stopped, went back, and then forward again.

"I'm not feeling well," he explained to his wife. "The events of the day have been a little too much for me. I want to go back. I have to see Stafford. It's about something very important."

"You spend a lot more time with Stafford than you do with us," complained Ruth.

"That may be, but perhaps sometime in the future things will be quiet again and then we can do what we want; perhaps we can even go and live in the old house on the deserted farm."

"I'd like that," commented Angelica.

Everybody had been working at full speed that day. The leaders had reached the point where they really wanted a rest. Even Stafford objected when Hubler insisted on an evening conference.

"You'd better rest, Paul," he advised.

"I can't. This is something that I have to get off my mind. We can't lose a minute. This may save our country. We have to talk it over."

"All right, but only an hour. These men will crack if we drive them too hard."

"I only want five minutes. If I can't put the idea over in five minutes, I'll be willing to say it's a bum one."

In an hour's time he was facing twenty of the most brilliant men in that part of America. There was no timepiece in that room, but there were hourglasses, filled with sand, which flowed from one glass container into another one.

Hubler placed a small sand glass on the center table.

"Gentlemen," he said. "There is an egg timer. It takes just that long to soft-boil an egg. And I'm going to take less than that time to give you my idea."

And the sand was still flowing when he paused.

The result of his few words was electrical. His idea was so simple that everyone wondered why someone hadn't thought of it before. The conversation was general, spontaneous, encouraging. Here was hope! Mankind from that moment ceased to grope in the dismal muck of despair, and began to return to the culture that once marked the height of the electrical age.

Six of the men worked on into the morning, but Hubler excused himself and returned to Ruth and Angelica.

"What did that man do before the crash, Stafford?" asked one of the scientists, as Paul left the room.

"I think he was a bank clerk of some kind."

"He seems to have a complete insight into every problem. He must have had an education out of the ordinary."

"I doubt it. He told me once that he never had a college education. But he read a lot, and the big thing he has is something that some of us lack…IMAGINATION."

During the next two weeks everyone worked hard at something. It was a peculiar period. In analyzing it later on, the interesting comment was made that during that time not a single written order was given. There was close harmony, complete cooperation between everyone. Everyone saw the peculiar work to be done which he or she was best fitted to do and then went and did it. At the end of ten days, Fort Telephone was well fitted to sustain a siege and all plans for the defense of the North Fence had been completed.

Stafford had been busy since his return from Pennsylvania. Without any intent on his part he had seen but little of the women he had brought with him from Shawnee. Others of the

Colony hadn't been so indifferent and already six of the women had married. The three Doctors, however, still remained single. One day, after the decision had been made to fight the battle out at the North Fence, Dr. Perno deliberately stopped Stafford on his front door steps.

"Good morning, Tiger Killer," she said.

"And the same to you, Man Killer," he retorted.

"Listen to me, Mr. Stafford. There is going to be a fight soon—"

"Not a fight, a battle!"

"Well, anyway, there are going to be a lot of men hurt. Have you arranged for a field hospital?"

"I think so. We have two male physicians who were told to look after the arrangements for the wounded."

"How about us three women?"

"You had better stay at Fort Telephone. There may be a lot of work for you there."

"We, at least I—well, anyway, I want to help back of the fence."

Stafford shook his head.

"You might get hurt," he said.

"What difference would that make? No one would care."

"Are you sure of that?"

The man and woman looked at each other. At last Stafford said, with a little smile: "These are bad times, Dr. Perno. No one can tell where any of us will be in a few weeks. If I were sure of the future, I'd like to talk to you about some things, but just now the kindest thing is to tell you to stay with the other women inside Fort Telephone."

Dr. Perno never replied. She simply turned and walked away. Stafford looked at her, somewhat puzzled.

He commented aloud, "I wonder what's the matter with that woman."

But other important matters claimed his immediate thought. Men were constantly coming to him for advice and suggestions. Messages had to be sent to this point and that. New arrivals had to be welcomed and arrangements made for their comfort, pending THE DAY. These new arrivals were interesting; they were all rather well educated men, and, independent of each other, had all arrived at the same place as far as their weapons were concerned. Axes of stone, bows and arrows, spears represented their walking arsenals. One group, a little one and the only one from Delaware, brought a catapult, on a cart. It was capable of throwing a hundred pound stone, but it took some time to load it. Against fortification it might be useful; but its effectiveness in fighting an enemy in the field was a question.

There was a great deal of discussion concerning the use of cavalry. Stafford was opposed to it.

"We're fighting," he said, "foes who are expert horsemen. Fighting from the saddle is second nature to them. If we went into them on horseback, we would be wiped out. I think that the place to keep our horses is back of the Fort. If we're defeated, the women and their guard might need those horses to escape to the West. I think that we have to do what we can on foot, and hope that our scientists will come through in time."

On the thirteenth day there was a general movement of the fighting force of the American army to the North Fence. Spies had told of the final approach of the Tartar tribe. All realized that the next day might tell the final story. There were only about a thousand men to defend the fence, and it was a long fence for that number to defend. Stafford hoped that the attack would come at one point and that they would be given sufficient warning as to where that point would be to concentrate there. He realized, and perhaps they all did, that if two thousand tartars stormed all of the fence at the same time, one thousand Americans would soon be dead. The leader wondered whether it would not have been best to leave a larger percent of his force behind the walls of the Fort. Only two hundred of the older men were there.

At the end of the thirteenth day, just as the sun was sinking, a new group of men joined the Americans. Stafford and his officers looked rather askance at the leader. He answered the unspoken questions, the ill-concealed antagonism.

"We're from Boston, and we're not what you call Americans. I can talk English, but most of my men talk any other language better. Most of us are from Sicily, and I know you don't like us. We used to be bootleggers and murderers and even white slavers, but when we left Boston, after the city broke, we took our women with us. We tried to behave ourselves, but everyone seemed to be afraid of us. We never had a break; so we kept on murdering. Then those Huns came and we had to run. They got our women. Understand? The girls are all dead now, but these killers have never paid for them. We have run before them, just waiting for the chance to collect what they owe us. Give us a chance, Mister."

"We'll give you a piece of the fence to defend," said Stafford. "You may not be our kind of Americans, but we're glad to have you with us. Perhaps, after the battle is over, we may understand each other better."

"We don't want to fight behind the fence," answered the man. "You fellows understand how to use those bows and arrows, but we have to fight the way we used to fight. We have knives. Understand? Knives. Just stone knives. But we know how to use them. And not one of us but has lost his woman and we want to collect."

"I think you'll have a chance," said Stafford kindly. "We'll send you some food and drink, and tomorrow you'll have the chance to use those knives."

It was dark. Sentinels were pacing the Stone Fence. Here and there along the four miles campfires were burning as though to show the world that here civilization was quietly preparing for its last stand against barbarism.

Stafford had a final talk with Hubler, who was to bear the responsibility of command until daybreak. Then he slowly walked down to where his horse was picketed. A hostler was petting the horse's nose and whispering to him. Absent minded, Stafford mounted the horse, spoke to it, and rode away.

"By-by, old Tiger Killer," whispered the hostler.

Stafford wheeled the horse around. "Is that you, Dr. Perno? You go right back to the Fort."

"Yes?" asked the voice, and there was a certain soft insolence in the tone. "Yes? Always good at bossing, aren't you? But this time nothing is going to happen. The three of us Medics are here and we're going to stay here, and we're going to do the work of three men and do it better than any three men could do it. You're going to need us, even if you won't admit it."

Stafford galloped off into the darkness.

CHAPTER TWENTY-ONE
The Battle of the North Fence

The next morning was clear. There was no fog, not even a haze over the meadow in front of the stone fence. The Tartars had camped on the far side of the little stream and there everything was activity. On the defensive side of the fence there was not much movement. It was Stafford's plan to keep the enemy in ignorance of the number and location of the Americans. The fence, nearly seven feet high, had been made a little higher in some places by the addition of large stones placed near each other to give loopholes for the bowmen.

The Delaware men had their catapult near the center of the defense. They were eager to try their strange weapon, but realized that the psychic shock would be greater than any actual damage done and that at the best but few casualties would result from each stone thrown. Still, they had the range accurately determined and were sure they could do some damage.

The Vermont men had been placed in the woods. That was really a place of honor, for there was no stone defense there, and the fighting would be man to man. The Green Mountain boys were anxious to show what they could do, and boasted that they could lick their weight in wild cats.

At the last moment, Stafford had sent one hundred married men back to Fort Telephone. That left less than a thousand to hold the fence. They were divided in groups of fifty, all except the men from Boston. They insisted in their purpose of holding the center of the line.

The morning was half gone when several hundred of the Tartars waded across the creek, came up the hill to within a hundred yards of the fence and then, breaking into small groups, began to shoot arrows into the air. They were expert shots. Soon the arrows began to drop from the air down just in back of the fence. However, the Americans had cause to be thankful for the height of the wall, for by pressing closely against the stone fence, the defenders were completely protected from the sky missiles.

Now two other groups crossed the creek and lined alongside of the first two hundred. All advanced until they were within fifty yards, of the wall. They began now to shoot for the openings in the top of the stone rampart. There was still no sound, no answering response of any kind from the Americans. The Tartars seemed puzzled. What was on the other side of the fence?

Several hundred more crossed the little creek then. There were at least a thousand Asiatics occupying an area an eighth of a mile wide on each side of the cement road that passed through the gate, but there was no gate left.

Stafford had given rigid orders that nothing was to be done without a signal from him. He appreciated the element of suspense, the value of surprise. The Americans held firm to his orders but the Boston bandits, already hyperemotional, were driven frantic, by the death of their leader. He had peered through a loophole just at the wrong second and died with a stone-pointed arrow in his forehead. They saw him fall, started cursing in Italian and the next minute the entire group, nearly a hundred, were over the fence and running down the meadow.

They were armed with nothing but their flint knives, twelve inches long, sharp as needles at the end, really terrible weapons for in-fighting. They had their left arms wrapped with blankets, intending to use them as shields. They were on the Tartars and into them before the men from Asia realized what was happening.

Stafford saw what the end was going to be. There could only be one answer, but in order to give the Bostonians what aid he could, he signaled for sharp shooting, careful, selective archery, with a definite target for every arrow. Each man within range was to shoot ten arrows and then stop. The signal was three long blasts on the ox horn.

The Sicilians ran into the men from Tartary and were at once engulfed. It was as though an amoeba had opened up, and, allowing a piece of food to enter, had once again closed its wall. There was not much noise, just a confused struggling, a tossing here and there and a gradual carrying of the entire mass toward the rivulet at the bottom of the slope. At last the fighting came to an end. The men from Boston, the Italian bootleggers, had joined their women, but in their journey they had carried with them the Asiatics. Days later when a careful estimate became possible, it was thought that at least three of the enemy had died for every Sicilian. It was at the most a gesture. In a spiritual sense, it was a supreme sacrifice magnificent in its futility.

Hubler stood by Stafford and watched the assault.

"How's the wind, Paul?" the chief asked, at the same time wetting his finger and holding it up in the air.

"It's wrong in two ways," answered Hubler. "In the first place it's blowing in the wrong direction and in the second place it's not strong enough."

"Yes, until the wind changes."

"I'd give anything for an airplane."

"Certainly, and so would I. No use wishing for the moon. Look! There goes a group on horseback headed for the woods. Must be at least fifty in that bunch. Shall we send help to the Vermont men?"

"I think not. They would be insulted. We need every man we have here. Mackson would be insulted. He said he would hold the woods. I think he meant it. Look there! That's one reason why we can't send help. This looks like a real charge."

It was. Fully a thousand Tartars were running up the cement road. They were going to break over the stone fence, and then spreading out turn back and wipe out the Americans. Stafford ordered the bugler to sound one long blast on the horn. It was the signal for concentration at a threatened point.

The Asiatics were massed. The Delaware men dropped three stones into them, each weighing a hundred pounds. The aim was perfect, but it was like dropping sand into a pond.

And now into the charging mass came the thudding arrows. No time or need for careful aiming. All that was necessary was to aim at the mass. Not an arrow missed a target. Still, they came on toward the wall, up on the wall and over it. Fifty yellow men dropped to the ground and started the Berserk fight with their stone hammers.

The Americans closed in on them, first with long spears, and later, as these broke, with hammer and tomahawk. It was hard, terrible combat; first one large group against another, then a lot of little groups and finally duelists.

Now came the sound of stone mutilating flesh, the sharp breathing of laboring men, the yell and gasp of the mortally wounded. At last it came to an end. The wall was safe. Hundreds of Tartars streamed back to their camp, but hundreds remained, the blood of Asia mingling in little pools with the best blood of America.

Stafford and Hubler, though leading the defense, came through unharmed. They rested on their axes, as they wiped the dripping sweat from faces, blood flecked from their silent enemies. They looked at each other and then at the meadow. A man came up.

"Wish to report that the Vermont men held the woods," he said, and then swaying slightly, dropped dead.

Hubler dropped to his knees and turned the man over.

"It's Mackson," he cried. "They held the woods but I guess they were wiped out in the doing of it."

"Oh! We're holding all right," commented Stafford. "We're holding, but I guess they have a thousand men that so far haven't started to fight. If they charge the fence again, it's going to be too bad—for us."

Hubler stood up, wet his finger and held it up toward the sky. For a minute he held it there and then dropped his hand.

"No change in the wind," he said.

"Then we might as well call the men closer together."

A man came up.

"We have no more arrows, Boss."

"Sound the horn for assembly. We must have three hundred men who have so far not shot an arrow. They'll have to join us."

"That will leave most of the fence unprotected," said the Head of the Delaware men, who had come up just in time to hear the conversation's end.

"We'll have to take a chance on that. If they flank us, we'll have to cut our way through to Fort Telephone. It will be better to fight in a mass than to be cut down piecemeal."

Just then a clap of thunder was heard. Black clouds began to form to the rear of the North Fence. A breeze began to blow.

"It's come," cried Hubler. "Just what we wanted. Now, if our boys can only come in time. If only it works!"

"It has to work!" replied Stafford. "See! The Tartars are forming for another charge. Their entire camp is beginning to cross the creek. Send the signal. An arrow into the air, carrying a white pennant. Quick. Hubler! I can't see you."

And Stafford dropped to the ground. Hubler was with him as he fell. A woman pushed him away.

"You fool!" she hissed. "Go and do what he told you to. I'll tend to him. Must be bleeding somewhere and never knew he was hurt. Probably would have died and nobody known it if he hadn't fainted."

And Dr. Perno started to find the bleeding point.

And at the same time the signal arrow blazed into the air, vivid against the blackness of the thunderclouds.

The Tartar tribe started up the meadow. All of them this time.

On the other side of the North Fence the Americans waited for the final test of strength; waited for what they felt was only one ending; hoping when every point of common sense told time that the time for optimism had come to an end.

Then from the mountaintop on the other side of the wood came something that looked like a vulture, and another and another, until twelve were soaring in the air. There was no beat of wings, simply a careful balancing against the air currents. They came lower and yet lower until they were between the two contending forces—some in the wide meadow between and some over the Asiatics. Now it could be seen that they were not birds, but men in gliding machines. And *from the gliders dropped death*.

The Tartars, puzzled, looked up in the air, wondered at what they saw, and too late, started to run. It was useless. On every gust of wind came the living death, curving in wreathing billows like fog from out the sea.

The yellow men ran and died. Most of them died before they came to the creek. The rest died trying to get under the water. In ten minutes it was all over. The flight of the Tartar tribe had come to an end. Starting nearly two years before in Gobi, it beat its last wing stroke at the base of the North Fence.

Once again intelligence had conquered over brute force.

From the top of the stone wall the American watched the debacle in perfect safety. A dozen of the leaders gathered around Hubler as though they expected him to say something. He did.

"It's not the big things in life, gentlemen, that count. I suppose that most decisive battles have been won by some accident, some little thing that no one thought about, like the sunken road at Waterloo. The thing that saved us today, that made America safe for civilization, was a sudden change in the wind. We couldn't have used the gliders had the wind not been strong enough to keep them in the air, and with the wind blowing as it did before the storm, we would have been killed by the poison gas instead of the Huns. I think the real heroes of the day were the men who used the gliders. Yes, I know we kept it a secret, but we were not at all sure of them, or whether we could use them, and we did not want to disappoint our men. They sailed nicely for crude construction, didn't they? We were lucky to find a lot of poison gas that had been stored in glass demijohns. We tied the demijohns upside down to the gliders and had ropes to the glass corks so they could be pulled out at the right time. It was a new gas the Army was going to experiment with just before the Metal Doom came. Suppose we stop talking and see if we can save any of our wounded?"

"That is all attended to," said Dr. Brown.

CHAPTER TWENTY-TWO
Wreckage

The survivors of the battle were tired, but there were men and women who had remained in Fort Telephone during the battle. These came, as soon as they could be sent for, and helped care for the wounded. Some could be saved but the wounds of a fight in the Stone Age were different from those in the age of steel, far more disabling and deadly. Yet even the hopelessly wounded were cared for by loving hands. Dr. Brown and Dr. Hufford directed the work of the little field hospital. Dr. Perno had disappeared with the stretcher-bearers who had carried Stafford off the field. It seemed that one patient was enough for her.

The field of battle on the other side of the fence could not be investigated.

The poison gas still hung in swirling wreaths and until it was all blown away no one could venture that way. But the leaders knew that all the Boston men were dead, and a search of the woods showed that all of the Green Mountain boys were dead except ten, and of these, five were fatally wounded. The Delaware men had lost twenty of their number. Pennsylvania had seventy who would never return and Stafford's colony had thirty dead. In the emergency hospital that was slowly being filled in one of the barns, over one hundred Americans were being cared for.

The American dead were buried in one long trench back of the fence they had so ably defended. That fence, four miles long, seven feet high and two feet wide was their only monument. During the next week, as soon as the meadow was safe, hundreds of men and horses hauled cordwood down to a large funeral pyre and there the men from Asia were burned. For days the flames, ascending to the skies, sent a message of victory to the western world.

Of the twelve men who had sailed the skies in the hastily constructed gliders, seven came to earth safely back of the American lines. The other five crashed to an earthly death but not until they had contributed their share to the victory.

A month after the battle there was little to show of what had happened. There was an acre of blackened meadowland, but that was later plowed up, harrowed and timothy sown. And there, for all the years to come, grew grass and clover richer than on any other of the Stafford fields. The men from Vermont, Maine, Delaware and Pennsylvania went back to their homes; some remained in a deep sleep by the North Fence and there shrubs were planted and blossoming flowers, and sweet smelling roses. Twenty years later the National Government made this battlefield a National Park and erected a memorial arch over the gateway, where the concrete road pierced the fence, and on the arch were carved the words:

"SUCH MEN CAN NEVER DIE, BUT LIVE ETERNAL HEROES"

There was work to be done, extra and unexpected tasks, but at last life returned to normal, and Hubler had time to spend with his family and Stafford.

The Chief had been badly hurt. There was no evidence external of the injury, but he had been struck by a stone ax on the head, a blow that must have been broken by his mat of hair and the leather cap he wore, yet which must have caused a severe concussion. He was asleep for several days and when he did awake he was moody and an extremely poor conversationalist. Everyone was worried about him. All missed his cheerful laugh and his kindly interest in the little things around him.

"You have to shake out of it, Stafford," urged Hubler. "The Doctor says that you're all right, and Dr. Brown says there is not a thing wrong with you—that you just think you're sick."

"These women Doctors interest me," the sick man replied. "Of course they've been wonderful. They tell me that Brown and Hufford worked miracles in the hospital, and even in the thick of the fight they were right there doing what they could for the wounded. But I just don't like a female Medico. Once a sick man gets in their hands they seem to think they own him in some way. I suppose it's the Mother instinct in them. I believe I should have been well by now if I had had a man treat me, but somehow when I dropped on the battlefield, Dr. Perno was right there and she has been in the same place ever since. She has been just as nice to me as can be, but I'm really tired of having her for my Doctor."

"Why not discharge her?"

"Yes? You know why. What has happened to the other women?"

"You mean those you brought from Shawnee?"

"Yes."

"They're all married. Dr. Brown was the last one to go. She had an interesting case, one of the Vermont men. She saved his life by some kind of an operation, and she was so interested in it that she married him. She said it would take a year to see how the operation turned out and she did not want to lose sight of him in the meantime; so, after the other Vermont men went back, this one stayed on and they were married yesterday. He is a real nice fellow, a college graduate and all that. So, they're all married now except Dr. Perno."

"I wish she would go and marry someone," sighed Stafford wearily. "Why don't you suggest it to her, Paul?"

"Not my business. Why don't you?"

"She might think I was growing personal. I tell you what I'm going to do. Wait a few days more until my head is a little clearer and then go away again. Too many people around here to suit me."

"I don't know where you would go where it's any quieter."

"I do. I bet this minute it's as quiet as can be right at 42nd and Broadway. That's the very idea. Always wanted to see what happened to little old New York since the crash and now I'm going to see for myself. Poor old Mackson told us about the curse of the cities but it may not be as bad as he described it."

"Going right away?"

"In a day or two."

"Don't go," pleaded Hubler earnestly. "Nothing there but wreckage!"

"Then that's the place for me. I think that I've made a mess of things. With you it's different; you have Ruth and the little one, and she's certainly a child to be proud of. But with me there's nothing worthwhile. I guess I was wreckage long before the Metal Doom, but civilization covered up the decay. When we got into the Stone Age I just couldn't make the grade. The other boys did, but I just seemed out of place. At times I felt like a disinterested spectator. I have had just one thrill in all these months and that was when I killed that tiger."

"Didn't it thrill you when those Tartars jumped over the wall? Or don't you remember it. I was too busy to watch you closely, but it looked as though you were having the time of your life."

"Honestly, Paul, I was bored. I tell you there's something wrong with me. I guess I'm crumbling into red dust, like the metals."

At that moment Dr. Perno came into the room.

"Here is your eggnog, Mr. Stafford."

"Just a piece of wreckage," sighed Stafford, as he drained the glass.

CHAPTER TWENTY-THREE
The End of a City

Three days later found Stafford tenting in Central Park. He was in a rather depressed state of mind. While essentially a rural-minded man, he had delighted in his occasional trips to New York City. The park had always fascinated him. The idea of acres of country surrounded by apartment houses whose penthouses almost pierced the clouds intrigued him. When he visited the Metropolis he never failed to spend at least several hours in the little oasis and practice his woodsmanship. To find some wild animal there, if only a skunk or chipmunk, was far greater sport to him than trailing the gold diggers of Broadway.

He had anticipated that the Park would be alive with humanity. At least he was confident that he would find some folks living there. In this thought he completely lost sight of the inability of the average New Yorker to adjust himself to any new situation. While he might be able to rapidly learn the mysteries of the Subway, he never would be able to learn the art of supporting life unless surrounded by cafeterias and delicatessen stores. So, while he found many evidences of past humanity in Central Park, he found no present inhabitants.

From the standpoint of housekeeping, the grounds were a pitiful mess. Thousands and hundreds of thousands of people had sought refuge there, abode for a while in makeshift tents and then, leaving most of their treasures, had wandered on in search of that greatest of all riches, food. Everywhere bones strewed the green grass, mute evidence of past tragedies and hungry dogs. All was chaos, disorder and ruin. Yet, nature was trying her best to restore her domain to its former beauty; the grass was tall, the trees green, and the flowers a riot of color.

On all sides of the Park were buildings in complete collapse. What interested Stafford was the fact that so much of this collapse had taken place internally; the buildings had apparently caved in and, while some of the debris had fallen into the streets, most of it had piled up on the sites of the former buildings. Had there been an accompanying earthquake, hurricane or even a period of high winds, the avenues would have been filled fifty feet high.

The wanderer found a part of the park that seemed cleaner than the rest and pitched his tent. His two horses were picketed and a fire built. Though he was apparently rather isolated, he took every precaution against surprise and attack. Night found a quiet city, except for the howling of distant dogs. The man wondered what had happened to the dogs of New York.

"More dogs than babies here in the Park the last time I was here," he commented to himself.

Towards dark he heard the sound of steps crashing through the weeds. He jumped back of the fire and prepared his bow and quiver of arrows for action. An old man came into view on the other side of the fire. At least he looked like an old man. He looked across the fire and saw the man with a bow and arrow ready in his hands.

"Don't shoot!" he cried. "I'm harmless."

"All right," responded Stafford, "but I'm taking no chances."

"That's right. But I live here in the Park. I've lived here since the trains stopped running."

"And I just came," said Stafford.

The two men sat down by the fire.

"My name is O'Connor," began the white-haired man, "And it's a name to be proud of. I lived over in Jersey, but I worked here in the city, and I used to spend my holidays in the Park. I liked it. Used to think that it belonged to me and hated to see the litter of newspapers and peanut shells and banana peels. Would spend hours picking things up and making the place tidy. When the rush came, the place was a mess. Might have been a million people here, and everything you could imagine in the way of property, and that, with the wild animals running around loose from the Zoo, made the pretty place a regular Inferno like the one Dante described. People went insane and bad in every way, and their sickness was as much spiritual as physical though many of them starved to death.

"I came up here and I stayed. Found a little cave and furnished it with the stuff people dropped, and then, after everybody left, I started to clean the place up. The litter was so thick that you could hardly step on a square yard of clean, healthy grass. I made a regular program of so many square yards a day and an extra allowance for Saturdays; because I never thought it right to work on Sunday. It was hard work, at least part of it, but I'm moving right along. Yes, indeed, and ten more years will see a nice clean park, believe me, Mr. Stafford."

"That's a remarkable story, Mr. O'Connor. And all by yourself all these months?"

"No. There's been lots of company. There were the dogs."

"Yes, I heard them tonight."

"Funny about them. They can't leave the city. Looks as though they were afraid to go into the country yet, it's hard to see what they live on—unless?"

"They hunt in packs, do they?"

"Yes, but I don't mind the dogs. When they come at night I'm in my cave. It's the Subway people I'm afraid of."

"But—didn't the Subways cave in?"

"I suppose some of them did, but much of the system must have held its shape. When the buildings began to give way, lots of people went down there. It must have been a dark, unholy hell for a while. Thousands of people down there of all kinds and all ages—in the dark—waiting for something to happen.

"I'm not sure what did happen. At times I get thinking about it until I nearly go mad and then I start gathering rubbish until I become calm again. But it was a survival of the fittest; not the best you understand, but the kind that were best able to fight it out and now there is a Bronx gang, and a Circle gang and a Times Square gang, and I suppose other gangs downtown and over the river."

"Not nice people, I guess," Stafford commented.

"No. Not at all nice. I've seen them pass over Central Park more than once and wanted to kill them, but what could I do? Yet, I have a plan, and some day I'm going to work it out."

"You don't seem to like them?"

"Not at all. If the dogs cut them off one at a time and eat them, it suits me. Dog eat dog."

"Where is your cave?" asked Stafford.

"Up the Drive a ways. Must have been there for centuries but no one knew about it. I happened to see a crack and worked around it, and first thing I knew I went inside. Nice little place; even has a spring of water."

"I bet it's clean," laughingly commented the man from the country.

"You bet it is. Come and see me tomorrow night. If you come before sundown, you won't have any trouble finding me. Perhaps you would consider living with me. This place here is bad—if the dogs come."

"How about my horses?"

"There's a fine place for them up on the rocks back of my cave."

"I may come. At least I thank you for the offer, and will think about it. I don't want to make you feel badly but I wanted to be by myself for a while, so I could think things over, and that's why I came here to the city; still, it's nice to have you call, and I want to keep in touch with you."

"I wish you would come," said the old man wistfully. "I have a real nice library."

"I'll use it," said Stafford as he said goodnight.

The next day the country man rummaged through the remnants of the Broadway shops. He found most in ruins and almost all looted. The following day he saddled one of the horses and rode up C.P. West. There were piles of debris on the city side of the street but there was a rather wide, clear space on the park side. As he started to turn west to find the O'Connor home, he saw a lone horseman come down the Avenue. He stopped, waiting for the man to come to him. At last the stranger came near enough to make recognition possible.

"Dr. Perno!" cried Stafford. "Whatever are you doing here?"

"Seeing the city."

"Did you know I had come here?"

"Of course not! You don't think I'd follow you, do you? I wanted to get some surgical supplies and we women talked it over and decided that I might as well come as anyone else."

"Since you're here," sighed Stafford, "I suppose I'll have to be nice to you. Suppose we call on O'Connor?"

CHAPTER TWENTY-FOUR
The End of O'Connor

"He is a friend of mine," explained Stafford. "We only met the other day but I liked him from the first. I may go and live with him. He said his cave was on the West Side. Suppose we ride in here and hunt for him? Likely find him at work; he has promised himself that he will clean up the park."

"Does it need cleaning?"

"It does. The whole city does. In fact, you have no business being here by yourself."

"I have always been able to take care of myself!"

"No doubt. But there are some parts of life in New York that wouldn't be very pleasant to you."

As they talked, they rode through the park. The part they saw was very clean. No doubt of the efficiency of O'Connor there. Dr. Perno remarked about it.

"In the old days it was never this clean."

"There is a part over there that the old man overlooked," answered Stafford, as he rode towards a peculiar mass at the foot of a tree.

He jumped off his horse and knelt beside it.

"It's O'Connor!" he gasped, "They've killed him."

The Doctor was instantly by his side, making a careful examination of the body."

"They didn't just kill him," she whispered.

"No. This is torture; it's the work of one of the Subway gangs. He was afraid of them and warned me against them. They must have caught him in a trap of some kind. He didn't have a chance for his life; he was not much of a fighter anyway."

"What are you going to do about it?" asked the woman.

"Bury him first, and then find his cave. And after that clean up the city."

"You mean the Subways?"

"Yes."

"How are you going to do that?"

"I don't know. The old man said he had a plan. Perhaps the cave will show what that plan is. He must have his tools there; so, suppose we find it and then come back?"

The cave was rather cleverly hidden. Stafford was a woodsman and a hunter and he simply tracked the foot treads until they ended in a cunningly concealed opening in a large rock. O'Connor had been right. The entrance was large enough to admit a horse and the cave itself was ample quarters for several persons and their belongings. It was cleanly and comfortably furnished. A fireplace and blackened rock showed that ample draught was provided by a crack in the wall. Everything necessary for comfort was in the large room; there were even luxuries in the form of books and pictures.

"When we see this place and realize what kind of a man those devils killed, it makes one more determined than ever to make them pay for it!" exclaimed Stafford.

Meanwhile Dr. Perno had been rummaging around. She cried. "Look at this stuff. Just like gray candles."

Stafford took a piece to the door to get a better light.

"It's dynamite," he commented. "Be careful of that candle of yours or you'll blow us all up. How much of this stuff is there?"

"At least a hundred pieces."

"That's what he meant when he said he had a plan. He was going to blow up their stairways, and let them die in the trap. I really think that when the time came, he wouldn't have been callous enough to do it. He was a gentle soul."

"Let's bury him," said Dr. Perno, "and let's plant some flowers on the grave."

They did so. It was nearly sundown when they finished.

"We better stay in the cave tonight," advised Stafford. "I tented out last night, but the danger is great. We'll stay here and I'll watch."

"We'll take turns," the physician insisted.

But Stafford insisted on guarding the entrance to the cave until daylight. Then he woke his companion and agreed to go to sleep for a few hours. It seemed only a few minutes of sleep, but in reality it was three hours when she woke him.

"There are a lot of men out there," she whispered. "I think they're trying to find the cave. They must have come back, found that the old man was buried and now they're hunting for the ones who buried him."

"Can you shoot?"

"Of course I can."

"Then let's get busy. But first I'm going to fix some fuses on a few sticks of dynamite. Ever light a giant firecracker and throw it so it explodes in the air?"

"Yes I used to do that."

"We'll try it if we get in a jam. Suppose we take our arrows and see what we can do?"

Crawling through the doorway, they hid behind the concealing shrubbery. About fifty men were walking around in front of them, evidently hunting something. A few were as close as twenty feet. They were a hard looking lot, and amid their laughter and curses they recalled the slaughter of the previous day and bragged about it.

That was more than Stafford could stand. Motioning to the woman to begin, he fitted an arrow to his bow, took careful aim and let fly. Almost at the same time Dr. Perno fired.

Six men were down before the gangsters knew what was going on. Then they started to run. Stafford came out, and kept on killing. It was clever archery, but in five minutes it was all over.

"Now, Doctor, you go in and get breakfast, and I'll go and recover our arrows. I'm not sure, but I believe the results will go toward proving that you're a good marksman, even if you do use 'little' arrows."

"I did all my practicing on birds and squirrels," she replied, "besides I know the vital parts. Anatomy is a useful study at times."

"You certainly are a peculiar woman!" Stafford laughed.

"It sounds nice to have you acknowledge that I *am* a woman," was her reply, "and now I'll get breakfast. I don't want to be around—when you get the arrows. And don't forget. They're going to come back."

"I expect that. And when they do, we'll be ready for them."

It was an hour before he entered the cave. His face was drawn and haggard. She looked at him inquiringly.

"Seventeen," he said in answer.

"All dead?"

"Yes."

He ate the meal she had prepared in silence and then, without a word, went and started to prepare the dynamite. Somewhere the old man had found the sticks and several hundred feet of fuse. The farmer understood dynamite. More than one day he had spent clearing land, blowing up tree stumps and large rocks. When he finished, he had all the dynamite arranged in three arcs around the mouth of the cave. The ends of the fuses were all bunched together over the cave.

"We're going to stay up here," he exclaimed. "It will be too dangerous in the cave. I'm going to take the horses back and hide them. We will hold the rock. They'll come here, find the cave, try to open the door, and then form a large crowd around the entrance. At least I hope they will. Then we'll set off the fireworks. We may have to fight for our lives after that, but I doubt it. I think they'll be too frightened to do much fighting."

The woman looked serious.

"I suppose you realize that you're planning to kill them without giving them a chance for their lives?" she asked.

"They've done that a thousand times to others. And they did it to my friend."

She sighed.

"This was a pretty place yesterday. It would have been a nice place to spend a vacation."

"We're going to spoil it," retorted Stafford.

"I'm not sure that I like you," cried the angry woman. "I believe you delight in making a mess out of things."

He pretended that he did not hear, but went off with the horses.

At noon the mob came, several hundred of them, murder in their hearts. No matter who had done the killing in the morning, they were going to do the killing in the afternoon. There were women in the crowd, brought on by the hope of finery or treasure. They had no trouble this time in finding the door to the cave. Opening it was another matter. The confusion was great. All of them crowded in, cursing and laughing and hunting for something to kill. Then came a hissing as of dozens of snakes. Some heard it and tried to listen; others saw the sparks in the grass and wondered why they were there.

AND THEN THE EARTH VOMITED.

Dr. Perno and the man lay on the overhanging rock and shut their eyes. Dust filled the air. Here and there were cries, but for the most part, there was an overwhelming silence. A few men ran off into the woods.

"Don't cry, Dotty," whispered Stafford, gathering the trembling woman into his arms.

"I can't help it John," she whispered through her tears. "I came to New York to find something, and now I want to leave."

"Did you find what you wanted?"

"I believe so. What did you come here for?"

"I'm not sure that I knew at the time, but I know now."

"Are you sure?"

"Positive."

That seemed to satisfy the woman.

At last she broke the silence.

"I hate the city. I want to get away from it as soon as possible."

"Where shall we go?"

"Why not go to Shawnee?"

"But all your friends are gone from there. We'd be alone."

"That's why I want to go there, stupid!" whispered Dotty.

CHAPTER TWENTY-FIVE
Honeymoon

John Stafford and Dotty Perno.

So satisfied were they with the richness of the new experience that had come into their lives, that they were willing to leave all of the wealth of New York for it.

Singly they had come into the great city. Together they had faced great danger and through that danger had been able to find the love they had for each other. Now they were leaving the ruined city together, feeling that nothing could ever part them.

They rode two horses and a third carried their belongings. The weather was beautiful, and once beyond the city, the country charmed them with its sweetness. Without conference, for they were at that period of life when they spontaneously arrived at the same conclusions without spoken contact, they slowly wore their way down to Port Jervis and from there down the Delaware River Valley to Shawnee. There was no reference made to the past. Every thing was just a foregone conclusion. At last they came to a familiar meadow and there part of the veil of illusion snapped.

"I hope," said Stafford, "that we can find another tiger."

"It looks hot enough," cried Dotty,
"to kill any germ."

¶ To many people it may sound like blas-
phemy to decry the advantages of our fast-
approaching thoroughly mechanized era.
But a great many others will realize the
seriousness and wisdom of Hubler's conten-
tions. At any rate, it cannot be denied that
already we are losing the fine art of living.

"I don't," exclaimed Dotty. "You were just lucky that day. Suppose that beast had killed you? Then what would have happened to me? The next tiger you meet I want you to turn your horse around and run for your life."

"You mean you don't want me to kill any more tigers?"

"That's it. No more tigers or bad men or anything. I simply want to forget there is such a thing as death. I've just found out what it means to live and I want to forget everything else for a long, long time. For years, maybe."

"Just want to be happy?"

"That's it."

"Looks as though we ought to be, up here on Hilltop."

The woman smiled as she looked at the man.

"Sure you'll be happy up here with me, John?" she asked.

"Certainly."

"Won't want to run away and spend the evening with Hubler and the other men?"

"I've forgotten they existed."

"Not sorry that we stopped at that nice old minister's house and were married?"

"Not at all, Dotty."

"Then we'll stay here forever, just the two of us."

"That suits me, Dotty."

"And there will never be a cloud in our life?"

"Not even a little one, except to shade you from the sun, or to make the sky more beautiful."

They came to the house of Dr. Perno. It was very much as they had left it months before. Everything was there; the flowers were a little wilder, the grass a little higher, the birds and squirrels somewhat tamer. Otherwise everything was the same. Up the valley, in the haze of twilight, the river lay—a silver streak amid the downy cushions of its protective meadows. To the south the Water Gap held up its twin mountains in majestic splendor throwing somber, ominous shadows into the darkening gulf between their mighty sides.

It was a pretty place to build a house.

Stafford took care of the horses and silently put their belongings in place, but the former Dr. Perno, the new Dotty Stafford, simply leaned against a pine tree and looked and looked at the country before her.

"I want to live here forever, John!" she cried.

CHAPTER TWENTY-SIX
A Woman Dies

It was a trifle cold that evening and after supper Stafford built a fire in the large open fireplace. The lovers sat in front of it in happy silence. At last the happy woman said. "Nothing can disturb our happiness."

But the man, listening, replied with a slight frown as he reached over for his stone ax. "I'm not so sure of that. There is someone coming up the walk."

And as he finished, a knocking was heard at the door, and a voice called, "Dr. Perno. Are you there?"

"She is here," answered Stafford. "Who are you and what do you want?"

"I just came down off the mountain. I need a Doctor and they told me there were women Doctors here and that one of them by the name of Doctor Perno lived in the old school house."

"Come right in," invited the woman. "What is the trouble?"

The man came up to the fire. He was a young man, very poorly dressed and shivering from the cold.

"I'm Peter Arndt, Madam, and I live up toward the Pocono. When things went wrong the girl and I talked it over and we thought that we would be happier if we were married, even though times were going to be hard. We had a log cabin a little off the road and neighbors were scarce, and none of the city folk came to bother us. Things went better than we had a right to expect, we were doing well and had a nice little herd of cattle, and then—we found there was going to be a baby. My wife's mother came to help and this morning she told me that there had to be a Doctor there—things were not going right—so, I saddled the horse and started out, and you're the first one I could find."

There was not a second's hesitation on the part of Dotty.

"Saddle the horses, John," she commanded.

Stafford went to obey her. She went to the closet and started looking over her medical armamentarium. It was not a very pleasing or promising investigation; some drugs, but absolutely nothing in the way of instruments. She started to frown, not at all pleased.

Ten minutes later the three were on their way to the home of Peter Arndt. It was a moonlit night, but even with the light from the full moon it was impossible to go faster than a walk. Daylight was breaking when the ride ended. Dr. Perno took her little bundle and went into the log cabin; the two men stayed outside with the horses; Arndt busied himself with feeding the stock and Stafford tried to help him. Neither man spoke of the drama being enacted inside the little home; it never occurred to either of them to go inside. The sun rose in the sky and was at last overhead. Arndt sat down on a rock.

"Times have changed," he remarked to Stafford. "Sometimes I don't seem to notice it much and then again it's mighty hard. All morning I've been wanting a knife, a real one, with a razor sharp blade."

"What for," asked Stafford.

"Just so I could whittle. Take a time like this and give a man a knife and a piece of old white pine and it's mighty comforting to sit and whittle."

Before Stafford could reply, his wife came out of the cabin. She looked old and very tired as she called her husband to one side. "I wish you would hunt around for some tools, John, and go up in the woods and dig a nice bed; cover it with golden rod and asters, and then, when you're ready come back," she said.

"Do you mean?" asked Stafford, in a whisper.

"Yes. Both of them."

"Shall I tell him?"

"No. I'll do that. It's part of my work."

Some hours later the two of them rode back to Hilltop, just above Shawnee. The ride was in silence; the supper was in silence. It was not until they sat out in the meadow that either spoke. Then it was Dotty who began:

"I never realized what the loss of metal meant to women before this, John."

"Just what do you mean, Dotty?"

"Simply this. Maternity is no longer a simple process; it has become a pathological condition, but we had such valuable aids in the metal age, instruments, hypodermics, surgical supplies of all kinds that we forgot that every child came into the world at a very definite danger to the mother's life. No doubt since we went into the Stone Age millions of mothers have died—only I didn't know about it, and didn't have the imagination that was necessary to visualize it.

"The condition last night was not an unusual one. In the old days with my filled obstetrical bag, I wouldn't have had a bit of trouble in saving both the mother and the child. But I was in the Stone Age. Think of it! The knowledge and science of the age and electricity and the instruments of twenty thousand years ago. There was nothing I could do. Absolutely nothing. So, I just sat there by the bed and watched her die.

"And she's just one of millions of women who are going to die, John. They're going to die, trying in a blind way to fulfill a biologic urge and perpetuate the race. Some will live and more will fail. And I was happy when we came to Hilltop and I never wanted to see anyone, just live on and on with you, and be happy, but I can't be happy now, because I won't be able to forget that woman and her little child.

"We have to have metal back into our lives, John Stafford. Not very much of it. We can do without gold and silver and platinum, and we don't need tons and tons of copper and steel; but we need a little, just enough to make a few instruments. Every community must have some, and someone who knows their use, because otherwise the culture and refinement and beauty of our race will die out.

"The savage, the barbarian will survive, but the women of intelligence will be unable to carry on the torch of existence. We'll either go childless or we'll die.

"We have to have metal. Not to build bridges, or airplanes, or ships; not for communication between continents; or for the manufacturing of mighty machinery, but just a little metal to make a few instruments, so our women can be saved.

"We love each other, John. And that love can only come in to its fullest power and beauty when we have a child, but I know—I'm sure of it after last night—that if I have a child, I will die, and I don't want to die. I don't want to leave you; life means too much to me, and I'm not sure that you would ever smile again if you went through what Peter Arndt went through today.

"So, if you love me, you will—in some way—find some metal. We can hammer it roughly with rocks. We can polish it with stone. Thus we can make tools with which to effect more things out of metal. Will you do it...for my sake? Find just a *little* metal?"

"I'll try," replied John Stafford.

CHAPTER TWENTY-SEVEN
A Lone Scientist Despairs

The selection of Mount Minsi as a scientific laboratory had in it all the elements of a grand despair. For thousands of centuries no one had ever thought of living on such a place. Now it held the home of one of America's foremost scientists.

Anthony Burke had back of him the traditions of all the great scientists of the world. He was as well versed in the history of invention as he was in the exact formulae of every intricate chemical or physical problem. As an apprentice he had served under a few of the great inventors of the electrical age. He had even contributed more than a mite to the final perfection of television.

Of all the great scientists of the world, he had arrived the earliest at a clear realization of what the red rust of metals would mean to civilization. He spent the first twenty-four hours following the destruction of the hairsprings in watches, in a careful, painstaking survey of the entire problem. After that he selected from his laboratory a collection of chemicals and instruments, all of an absolutely non-metallic nature. He presumed, and rightly so, that a physical condition affecting one metal, steel, would in time affect all metals.

His next step was the selection of a site for a workshop and the transportation of his scientific equipment. Not being a sociologist, he had a clearer idea of the effect of the Metal doom on machinery than on the human soul. Realizing this personal deficiency, he called on a student of human behavior and asked for an approximate description of what would happen to the structure of human society under the new conditions. A few hours with this man convinced him that life as it had been under former surroundings would become extremely difficult and all scientific study an utter impossibility. He determined to seek isolation.

On the third day of the new era he was spending all his wealth for the accomplishment of two purposes. One was the building of a stone house on the top of Mount Minsi; the second was the transportation of his scientific apparatus and supplies to that house. He spent his money like water, realizing that the time was rapidly approaching when it would be more worthless than water. The people of the Water Gap were glad to take his money, and to do his work for him, though they considered him insane.

Toward the end of the building operations, he had to work alone, but the final result was rather satisfactory. He had a substantial two-room house, stone walls, a wooden rooftree, and a slate roof. There was a fireplace, as well as ample light from windows. One room he used for living in, the other to work in.

There he determined to stay in splendid isolation and to redeem mankind from the curse of the second Stone Age.

He spent the first year of his study in an endeavor to rebuild his instruments of precision, which had been wrecked by the destruction of their metal parts. He felt the study of the disease that had wrought such havoc among the metals of the world could only be accomplished by the use of a well-equipped lab, and this he sought to organize. At the end of the year he had been able to prepare some metallic-like substances out of organic materials, such as casein and cellulose, but the shaping and utilization of such materials without instruments was more than even his trained mind could elucidate. At the end of the year he had built a workable scale and a very simple microscope.

All through this effort to determine the nature of the Metal Doom he was tormented by the knowledge that he was the first great scientist who had tried to work in a stone age. For thousands of years, all the great students and inventors had been aided by instruments of metal. More and more they had come to depend on these instruments, fingers of steel, arms of copper, brass and bronze. Everything they did, everything they thought, was tensely and tightly connected with the mineral kingdom. Ben Franklin may have thought of harnessing the electricity from the clouds, but he needed a metallic key to aid him.

Anthony Burke placed the primitive scales and microscope on a table and spent long hours, lonely days, desperate months in front of them, dreaming of the past greatness of his profession. He thought of his wonderful predecessors, the masters of the past, took up each of their great inventions, and wondered how they would have proceeded, what they would have accomplished, and how they would have reacted to their failures if they had been forced to work in an age of stone.

And he saw, or thought he saw, that man had risen from the ape, because he had learned the use of minerals. That, and the utilization of fire, had opened a great void between the human and the animal, had made the one a demigod and the other a howling quadruped, digging groundnuts and forgetting from one minute to the next, the determination of the moment past.

He felt, though in that he was obviously wrong, that a race, deprived of metals, would sink back into the past levels of anthropological life. Fire remained, but perhaps even that would some day be remembered vaguely as one of the last of the great arts.

Anthony Burke passed into the third year of his isolation a miserable mystic. At times he felt that insanity would end his problems for him. He became mentally stagnant. Spiritually he was simply a scientist in despair.

CHAPTER TWENTY-EIGHT
A Celebrated Picnic

"I want to propose something, Dotty," said John Stafford to his wife. "Let's go back to the colony and talk things over with Hubler. There's a fellow that has imagination. I bet that if you talk to him about the need of metal instruments the way you talked to me the other night, he will just imagine some way of making use of something or other to help you out. Now, I'm just a farmer, sort of a New York cowboy, but he had real ability."

"But I want you to get the credit for the discovery, John."

"That's nice of you, but I'm simply not talented that way. We'll go and see Hubler. But first we're going to have a picnic. What do you say to our climbing Mount Minsi?"

"That would be some climb, John."

"Sure would. I bet no one has been up it since the day the world went smash: Only lovers and fools ever climbed it anyway in the old days and now there is less reason to go to the top than there ever was. So, let's take some lunch and make a day of it, and if we get to the top late in the day, suppose we stay all night and see the sunrise from the top."

"I believe I'd like that," answered Mrs. Stafford.

The climbing of Mount Minsi would have been considered child's play by the experienced Alpine mountaineer. The ascent is gradual, and even in the steepest part there is no decided element of danger. The walk, in the old days, was interrupted by various pleasure houses, built at promontories carefully selected for the splendor of the view at various points. These offered resting places for the tired vacationist. After the advent of the automobile and the decline of the pedestrian, few dared the entire climb. In late years a survey of the Gap from an airplane had become a satisfactory substitute for walking to the top of Minsi. After the early days of the second Stone Age no one had ventured to the summit. The inventor had been left in isolated solitude.

To Stafford and his bride, alive with the joy of life, the conquest of the summit offered no difficulties. Leaving their horses at the first promontory, they arrived at the top of the mountain at the end of a brisk three hours walk. The view from either direction was only limited by the optical deficiencies of the human eye; the beauty of it was beyond words.

But the greatest thrill of the day came when they saw a stone house perched on the highest part of the mountain, and smoke coming from the chimney of that house. A house—fire! These could mean nothing but human habitation.

"I think we ought to call on him," suggested Stafford.

"How do you know it's a him? It might be a her," countered Dotty.

"I don't think so. No woman would live up here."

"She might if there was a man up here and he loved her."

But by that time Stafford had walked up to the door and knocked on it. Always the careful, prepared barbarian, he had one hand behind his back and in that hand was a small but very sharp tomahawk.

A small man with long, disordered, white hair and soiled clothes came to the door.

"Well?" he asked. "Who are you and what do you want?"

"I'm John Stafford and this is my wife. We were climbing the mountain, wanted to have a picnic dinner up here, and we saw your house and the smoke and thought we would come over here and have you join us. I mean we should like to have you share our lunch with us."

The white-haired man trembled with excitement.

"You will have to excuse my actions," he explained. "I've lived up here for over two years and you are the first people who have come to see me; in fact, you are the first ones I've spoken to in all that time. Living by myself, without any company and worried like I am, has made me a little queer. I would ask you to come in, but you know how a place looks when there is no woman around to look after things. My name is Anthony Burke."

But right there Dotty interrupted him.

"Not the Anthony Burke who invented the magneto amplifier for the latest model of the Tesla Television Cabinet?" she asked.

"Yes. I did that. At least, they named it after me."

There was no mistaking the admiration in the young woman's eyes. They fairly glistened as she continued.

"Then you're the very man I want to see. I've known about you for years. You had the reputation of being one of America's greatest scientists. After the world crashed we often talked about you and wondered what had happened to you. I don't know what you have been doing, but I know what I want you to do. Can't you somehow make some metal for me? Something that's hard and can be worked into different shapes and given a polish? I don't care what kind of metal it is, just so it can be used to make instruments with. Have you thought about it? Do you realize that women are dying every day because we're in an age of stone? Won't you please use your ability and do something, something for the women in the world and the little babies?"

The man started to cry. He wiped his face with his sleeve.

"That's what I've been working on for over two years," he sighed. "For over two years, and I've accomplished nothing."

"Let's have our picnic lunch," interrupted Stafford. "You'll feel better when you eat one of Mrs. Stafford's meals."

CHAPTER TWENTY-NINE
An Inspiration

Stafford and his bride tried to throw an atmosphere of good cheer and happiness over the lunch. They felt the inventor was rather morbid, that he had been alone so much, with nothing but failure for company, that he had become almost psychotic. Dotty particularly endeavored to cheer him and even went so far as to tell a few funny stories. Anthony Burke refused to laugh, but at last he passed the stage of disconnected sentences and became able to take an appreciable part in the conversation.

"Something had to happen to humanity," he remarked.

"You think," said Stafford, "that if it hadn't been the Metal Doom, it would have been something else just as terrible?"

"I believe so. You see, the human race was drifting into a mental and spiritual condition that was rapidly making continuance of life on a large scale impossible. Many peculiar and abnormal things happened after the World War. All of the human race was sick.

"There was a marked decline in the moral concept of right and wrong. Everybody became twisted in their thinking. Russia went socialist. The United States, with the control of the world's gold in her hand, went into an emotional, financial panic, and had over ten million out of work and starving. Then, with wheat at thirty cents and cotton at six cents, her economists favored the destruction of the surplus of both crops to raise the price while millions were starving and freezing for the lack of these staples.

"At the same time the people were attending amusements by the millions. Everybody was driving an automobile; the working day was shortened, the working week was curtailed, wages were going up, good positions fewer, people had more leisure than they knew what to do with, the racketeers ruled the cities, and the worthwhile people did not care enough to vote them out of power. Crime ruled, vice flourished, poverty increased. The rich became richer, the poor poorer, the more a man made the more he spent and nobody counted his change."

"Stop!" cried Mrs. Stafford. "Your indictment of society is too terrible. There were some good people before the crash."

"Of course there were," answered Stafford. "But what Mr. Burke is trying to show is that the good people were either not strong enough or sufficiently interested in the welfare of the human race to secure control."

"That's it," answered the inventor. "In thinking it all over, it seems to me that civilization was sick; and it was a rather unpleasant illness. There was something about it that just seemed as though it had grown so fast that its elemental parts could no longer function and that it was bound to decay. Something had to happen, and it did."

"Perhaps it was a good thing," mused Stafford. "Society was sick. Perhaps it had all kinds of spiritual bacteria working on it. Evidently it had reached a point where it could not bring about its own cure. But something had to happen, and I have been all through the change and I believe, Mr. Burke, that when we recover from this illness we're not going to be as sick as we were. We're going to be more unselfish; our vision is going to be clearer. Our value of events is going to be more perfect; little things are not going to upset us so; we're going to be nicer, kinder people than we were, and if the time ever comes when we're able to form some kind of government, it will be a better form of republic than the one whose death we have seen. Of course, there has been a lot of suffering, but it may be that out of it will come something worthwhile."

"What John is trying to say," explained his wife, "is that the same thing has happened to the human race that happens to an individual when they are very sick. If he recovers, his health is better than before. I'm not much of a scientist, but perhaps you can understand our meaning if I tell you that it's just as if the world were purified or sterilized by—by fire; that's what I'm trying to say, sterilized by fire and all the impurities and dross and germs burned out and nothing left but pure gold."

"And the red rust, the Metal doom, was just a means to an end; it was just a symbol. The metals became sick and collapsed, just as humanity did."

Stafford looked up the valley, and then he looked across to Mount Taminy. He took a deep breath.

"I'm just an ordinary farmer," he said at last, "but it seems to me there is an idea there in what Dotty is saying. If the metals were sick, perhaps they could be cured by fire."

Anthony Burke sprang into the air as though touched with an electric current.

"That's it! Oh—why couldn't I have thought of it myself? I had fire all the time. Common sense ought to have told me. And I had to wait until a farmer and his wife pointed the way. Perhaps it will work and perhaps it won't, but at least it ought to be tried. Until we do try, we won't know. Mr. Stafford, you and your wife go and get your things and come up here and live with me and help me. You have to be in on this. It's your suggestion. Fire... Oh hurry! I can't wait till I get started."

CHAPTER THIRTY
A Little Piece of Iron

Stafford left Dotty up on the mountain with the old inventor, while he went back to Hilltop. Returning, he brought the three horses well laden with necessities of life. After a night's sleep and a well-prepared breakfast, perhaps the most satisfactory meal the scientist had eaten for months, the two men started to prepare a furnace, while the interested woman looked on.

Burke realized he would need a high degree of heat. For fuel he had coal, charcoal and wood. None would give sufficient heat without a forced draft; so the first thing necessary was a bellows. A bellows of wood and skins was not the easiest thing in the world to make. Thus, the first day passed with little or nothing accomplished. A week likewise went by. In fact, it was a month before the crude furnace was made. The chimney was of stone and cement, the fuel was anthracite, and a porcelain crucible properly placed above the fire was to hold the red rust.

Stafford and the inventor had made a special trip to the D. L. and W. tracks to gather the red rust. The porcelain vessel was filled with this heavy powder; in fact, it was packed in as tightly as possible. Then the opening into the furnace was closed with stone and clay, and the fire underneath started. Stafford and Burke took turns at the handle of the bellows, and there was no doubt about the heat that was being generated.

"It looks hot enough," cried Dotty, "to kill any germ."

At the end of three hours the fire died away. There was nothing to do now except to let the furnace cool off and break it open. Anxious hours followed. At last Stafford took his stone ax and carefully smashed out a hole in the furnace. There was the porcelain pot, blackened but unbroken. It was still too hot to touch. They had no way of taking it out and they could not see what was inside it.

"I can't wait!" cried the inventor.

"You're just like a child before Christmas," laughed Dotty. "Come and eat your supper."

The next day they pulled the porcelain pot out of the furnace. The red rust was gone and in its place, at the bottom of the vessel, was a mass of a black substance that had a peculiar glisten to it.

"The metallic luster," cried Burke. "It looks like iron; it feels like iron, pure iron."

He turned the crucible over and the piece of metal dropped out. Stafford caught it before it touched the ground.

"It bends," he commented.

"It's malleable," commented the scientist. "Get me your stone ax. See! I can pound it into shape."

"I wanted it to be hard," complained Dotty.

"We can harden it. We can do anything with it that we used to. The important thing is that we have it. And if we have iron redeemed from the red rust, we can do the same thing with copper and gold and nickel and tin. We can make brass as Tubal Cain did. All we need now is an anvil and something to hold the piece of iron with and then we can do anything. We can make tools, and, once we can make tools, we can go on and redeem society. Think of it! Stafford. *We're out of the Stone Age.* One experiment, one success, *one little piece of iron marks the transition* into the new age of metals."

"I want you to hurry up and make my instruments," urged Dotty, now more than ever the old Dr. Perno; and yet, she was not the woman of the past. "Make your tools as fast as you can and then make some steel. Women are dying every day, and it may be my turn to die some day."

CHAPTER THIRTY-ONE
The Metal Workers

The piece of iron made on top of Mount Minsi is one of the most valuable possessions of the new Republic. Its recovery from the red rust of the D. L. and W. railroad tracks marked the end of the Second Stone Age.

Men had recovered the use of metals, but, though they were free from the tyranny of stone, they were still poor, as far as the abundance of all metals was concerned. The red rust was reclaimed as fast as possible, but it took a large amount to make even a little piece of healthy metal. When the mines were again worked, it was found that the metal ores under the surface had also been affected. Consequently, the world emerged into an age where every piece of iron; copper or tin, was of the greatest value. In fact, one of the earliest laws of the new nation was one regulating the use of metal and allowing it to be used only for certain definite purposes which would serve best the good of the national life.

The news spread. The idea was so simple, the technique so easily learned that soon all the little colonies were reclaiming metals from the red rust. They soon found, however, that it was one thing to obtain the metals and another to work them into valuable form. Metal workers, who understood the hand-working at the forge, the hammering of a hot piece of metal into a horseshoe, or the tempering of a piece of steel until it was able to take a razor edge, were few. For fifty years man had worked on metals with machinery instead of with his hands. Now there was no machinery. Everything had to start at the beginning. There was no essential difference between the metallurgy of the Phoenicians and that of the members of the Stafford Colony. Perhaps the men of Typre and Sidon were more expert.

With the reclamation of metals came new courage. Thinkers realized that it would be long before the old civilization was restored; the great leaders weren't sure it was worth the effort to bring it back. Mankind had learned the lesson of false values, of fictitious wealth, of cruel monopolies. There was bound to come a reaction, an effort to once more use the great inventions of the past, but with this determination came another thought, that much of the hardness of life that had come with the age of electrical machinery must be avoided in the new metal age.

The desire to work with the metals was overpowering and universal. No matter what else a man or woman could do, he or she wanted to make something out of iron, copper, or tin. During the months of deprivation, humanity had been hungry for the little pieces of metal that everyone had taken for granted for hundreds of years. To a woman, the making of a needle, the gradual sharpening and polishing and the laborious boring of the eye seemed to be the greatest cause of happiness, and once it was made and threaded and sewed with, there came a great sense of accomplishment. In the same way, the men worked to make knives, hinges for doors, forks to roast meat on.

Gradually, as the metallic necessities of life were obtained, scientists began to restore, in the simplest ways, the mechanical greatness of the former age. The population was so reduced, the poverty of material things so great, that it was realized that mass production would take years to materialize, but the great men wanted to leave a record of the past, while that record was still fresh in the memory of the living generation. Thus, one set of men built an automobile, another a typewriter, while a third group cut out type and began a crude printing press. The most interesting feature of communication was the complete loss of interest in the telephone and telegraph and the frantic effort to manufacture and put into use wireless. Within a year each little community had the ability to send and receive messages.

With the restoration of rapid communication came a rapid renewal of the bond of sympathy between separated groups. Men talked of the possibility of restoration of state and national government. While the intensive centralization of the past was to be avoided it was felt necessary to have the entire United States in close touch. It would never be the old nation, but the thinkers hoped that it would be a better one. Mackson's Constitution was taken out of the pigeonhole and carefully considered. It became the foundation for the new Government.

From the first, a constant effort was made to avoid the economic and social errors of the past. It was realized that there existed a profound functional difference between men, that some would be industrious and others indolent, some become wealthy and others remain poor, some achieve a high intelligence while others would remain morons. But all the colonies decided that every man, so long as he obeyed certain ethical commandments, had a right to the necessities of life. There would remain hardships but no poverty. Luxuries but no men of super wealth. The gulf between rich and poor was wiped out. At the same time the right of the individual to live his own life was respected. He could live as he pleased and work as he pleased, so long as he contributed a substantial tribute to the public welfare.

The underlying thought was that there should come the greatest benefit from the new metal age with none of the previous hardness of life.

CHAPTER THIRTY-TWO
The Curtain Drops

"Your husband," Stafford remarked to Ruth Hubler, "has become one of the great men of the new era. I believe he could be the first President of the new Republic if he were ambitious for honor. It was all due to his imagination."

Ruth sighed. "Even with his great imagination," she said, "I feel sure that he never was able to imagine how lonely Angelica and I have been for his company. Of course, I wanted him to do all he could for the Stafford Colony, but it does seem as though he might be able to spend a little time with his family."

"You ought to be proud of him, dear," said Mrs. Stafford.

"Oh! I suppose so. Come, Angelica, say goodbye to the twins and we'll go home."

So, they said goodbye to John and Dotty Stafford and the two little Stafford babies and went to their home.

There was no doubt that Paul Hubler had been away from home a great deal. Pleading business and important engagements, he often left early in the morning and did not come back until Angelica was asleep. The little girl was not sure at times as to whether she really had a father or not.

The Stafford Colony was a flourishing one. From the first it had possessed a number of well-educated people who, in addition to their intelligence, were blessed with common sense. The women who had come from Shawnee had all married. In fact, there was not one bachelor or old maid in the colony. The health of the community was excellent and the large number of sturdy babies gave promise of a wonderful future. Already plans were being made for the opening of a community school.

Dotty Stafford had attained her desire. The little ten-bed hospital was equipped with all the instruments needed to care for the emergencies of the Colony. From the day the first piece of iron was made she worked intently on this problem. The instruments she had made were not the beautiful polished tools of the past era but they were far better than the nothingness of the Second Stone Age. To the credit of her determination it can be said that no more women or children died for lack of proper care. Her husband felt that she was more of a doctor than she was a wife, but had to admit that she made a wonderful mother.

One morning Hubler actually slept late and had breakfast with his family. As a further surprise, he told them at the breakfast table that they were all going on a vacation, and that he would be ready to start right after dinner if they had their clothes packed. To show them he was in earnest, he drove around in a two-wheel cart, and tying the horse to the post in front of the house, started to help carry out the bags.

They had a cold dinner and then started off. Ruth and the little girl rode in the cart on top of the bundles of clothes and bedding, while Hubler walked in front of the horse, his stone lance in hand and his bow and arrows slung on his back. He was one of the men who clung rather lovingly to the weapons that had served him so well in the dark days of the past.

It was fall. The roads were covered with autumn leaves. Ruth made a coronet of the brown and golden beauties for Angelica. They had a merry time, and the two women so thoroughly enjoyed themselves that it was not until the horse stopped and the husband announced the end of the trip that they realized where they were. And then Ruth gasped.

They were back at the old farm, back to the house that had sheltered them on that momentous escapade, when they had fled from the city of ruined hopes.

They were back home!

The house had been repaired; the door no longer sagged but swung on three sturdy iron hinges; the roof was like new. The fences were in perfect order and the gates were perfectly grand. Two cows grazed lazily in the meadow and there was a goat and a kid. The little barn was swept and in order and the spring of water was singing a song of welcome. The happy woman jumped from the cart and ran into the house. Everything was clean, a polished kettle hung over the wood in the fireplace. All that was necessary was to start a fire and begin to cook supper.

"It's perfect!" she gasped to her husband who had followed her into the room. "Who ever did it all?"

"I did. At least most of it. I've been spending my days here for ever so long. You see, I wanted to surprise you."

"And are we going to live here, Daddy?"

"You bet we are."

"We're going to be happy!" cried Ruth. "It will be just like living in the dear old Stone Age all over again."

"Exactly!" agreed Hubler. "We'll have all the happiness of the Stone Age and most of the conveniences of the metal age. If the disaster served no other purpose, it at least drove us out of the city. Everybody is happier if he can plant his feet on old Mother Earth, and I hope that never again will cities rise as they did in the past, giant beehives, where all individualism was crushed and where the struggle for existence overshadowed the really worthwhile parts of life."

They had a wonderful afternoon and a delightful supper. Just as they were clearing up the dishes, they heard a sound of shouting down the road. From force of habit Hubler jumped for his stone ax. It was needless.

The People of the Stafford Colony had come for a house warming. They stayed to spend the evening. There were speeches and singing. At last Stafford spoke.

"We have come here tonight to ask a favor of you, Paul Hubler," he said. "Will you go to Washington as our representative?"

Hubler shook his head, but Stafford insisted:

"You must go. We need you there. Your wonderful imagination will be of value to the new nation."

"It is kind of you to ask me," replied Paul Hubler, "but I can't imagine Ruth and Angelica could possibly get along without me."

THE END

If you've enjoyed this book, you will not want to miss these terrific titles...

ARMCHAIR SCI-FI & HORROR DOUBLE NOVELS, $12.95 each

D-31 **A HOAX IN TIME** by Keith Laumer
INSIDE EARTH by Poul Anderson

D-32 **TERROR STATION** by Dwight V. Swain
THE WEAPON FROM ETERNITY by Dwight V. Swain

D-33 **THE SHIP FROM INFINITY** by Edmond Hamilton
TAKEOFF by C. M. Kornbluth

D-34 **THE METAL DOOM** by David H. Keller
TWELVE TIMES ZERO by Howard Browne

D-35 **HUNTERS OUT OF SPACE** by Joseph Kelleam
INVASION FROM THE DEEP by Paul W. Fairman,

D-36 **THE BEES OF DEATH** by Robert Moore Williams
A PLAGUE OF PYTHONS by Frederick Pohl

D-37 **THE LORDS OF QUARMALL** by Fritz Leiber and Harry Fischer
BEACON TO ELSEWHERE by James H. Schmitz

D-38 **BEYOND PLUTO** by John S. Campbell
ARTERY OF FIRE by Thomas N. Scortia

D-39 **SPECIAL DELIVERY** by Kris Neville
NO TIME FOR TOFFEE by Charles F. Meyers

D-40 **RECALLED TO LIFE** by Robert Silverberg
JUNGLE IN THE SKY by Milton Lesser

ARMCHAIR SCIENCE FICTION CLASSICS, $12.95 each

C-10 **MARS IS MY DESTINATION**
by Frank Belknap Long

C-11 **SPACE PLAGUE**
by George O. Smith

C-12 **SO SHALL YE REAP**
by Rog Phillips

ARMCHAIR SCI-FI & HORROR GEMS SERIES, $12.95 each

G-3 **SCIENCE FICTION GEMS, Vol. Two**
James Blish and others

G-4 **HORROR GEMS, Vol. Two**
Joseph Payne Brennan and others

A MURDERESS FROM BEYOND EARTH

His name was Kirk, and he spilled out the craziest story the local cops had ever heard from anyone undergoing a hard core police grilling. After all, who in their right mind could believe that a strange dame had come out of nowhere, clubbed a couple of people to death, and then promptly disappeared into a ball of blue light? Yeah…it was a tough story for any cop to swallow, and Kirk knew there wasn't much of a chance that he could beat the rap on a wild tale like this…

What the cops didn't know about this love-triangle murder mystery (garishly splashed all over the headlines of the local newspapers) was that the real answer to the mystery lay hundreds of thousands of light years away.

ABOUT HOWARD BROWNE

Howard Browne…

…was best known as a science fiction writer and editor. Browne was a mainstay at Ziff-Davis Publishing during the 1940s, working closely alongside then editor of *Amazing Stories* and *Fantastic Adventures*, Ray Palmer. When Palmer left in 1949, the editorship of both magazines passed on to Browne, who helped the magazines make the transition from pulp to digest publications. He also tried a more serious approach to the fiction in both magazines and ended Palmer's long association with Richard Shaver and his "Shaver Mystery" series of stories. Browne was a top writer of science fiction. Many of his works, like *Forgotten Worlds* and *The Man From Yesterday,* were written under various pseudonyms. During his career Browne was also known as a mystery writer, as well as for his work in television. He was born in 1908 and passed away in 1999.

TWELVE TIMES ZERO

By
HOWARD BROWNE

ARMCHAIR FICTION
PO Box 4369, Medford, Oregon   97501-0168

CHAPTER ONE

They brought him into one of the basement rooms. He moved slowly and with a kind of painful dignity, as a man moves on his way to the firing squad. A rumpled shock of black hair pointed up the extreme pallor of a gaunt face, empty at the moment of all expression. Harsh light from an overhead fixture winked back from tiny beads of perspiration dotting the waxen skin of his forehead.

The three men with him watched him out of faces as expressionless as his own. They were ordinary men who wore ordinary clothing in an ordinary way, yet in the way they moved and in the way they stood you knew they were hard men who were in a hard and largely unpleasant business.

One of them motioned casually toward a straight-backed chair almost exactly in the center of the room. "Sit there, Cordell," he said.

A quiet voice, not especially deep, yet it seemed to bounce off the painted concrete walls.

Wordless, the young man obeyed. Sitting, he seemed as stiff and uncompromising as before. The man who had spoken made a vague gesture and the overhead light went out, replaced simultaneously by strong rays from a spotlight aimed full at the eyes of the seated figure. Involuntarily the young man's head turned aside to avoid the searing brilliance, but a hand came out of the wall of darkness and jerked it back again.

"Just to remind you," the quiet voice continued conversationally, "I'm Detective Lieutenant Kirk, Homicide Bureau." A pair of hands thrust a second chair toward the circle of light. Kirk swung it around and dropped onto the

Police grilled him mercilessly, while eyes from a hundred worlds looked on.

seat, resting his arms along the back, facing the man across a distance of hardly more than inches.

In the pitiless glare of the spotlight Cordell's cheekbones stood out sharply, and under his deepset eyes were dark smudges of exhaustion. His rigid posture, his blank expression, his silence—these seemed not so much indications of defiance as they did the result of some terrible and deep-seated shock.

"Let's go over it again, Cordell," Kirk said.

The young man swallowed audibly against the silence. One of his hands twitched, came up almost to his face as though to shield his eyes, then dropped limply back, "That light—" he mumbled.

"—stays on," Kirk said briskly. "The quicker you tell us the answers, the quicker we all relax. Okay?"

Cordell shook his head numbly, not so much in negation as an effort to clear the fog from his tortured mind. "I told you," he cried hoarsely. "What more do you want? Yesterday I told you the whole thing." His voice began to border on hysteria. "What good's my trying to tell you if you won't listen? How's a guy supposed—"

"Then try telling it straight!" Kirk snapped. "You think you're fooling around with half-wits? Sure; you told us. A crazy pack of goof-ball dreams about a blonde babe clubbing two grown people to death, then disappearing in a ball of blue light! You figure on copping a plea on insanity?"

"It's the truth!" Cordell shouted. "As God hears me, it's true!" Suddenly he buried his face in his hands and long tearing sobs shook his slender frame.

One of the other men reached out as though to drag the young man's face back into the withering rays of the spotlight, but Kirk motioned him away. Without haste the Lieutenant fished a cigar from the breast pocket of his coat and began almost leisurely to strip away its cellophane wrapper. A kitchen match burst into flame under the flick of a thumb nail and a cloud of blue tobacco smoke writhed into the cone of hot light.

"Cordell," Kirk said mildly.

Slowly the young man's shoulders stopped their shaking, and after a long moment his wan, tear-stained face came back into the light. "I—I'm sorry," he mumbled.

Kirk waved away the layer of smoke hanging between them. He said wearily, "Let's try it once more. Step by step. Maybe this time…" He let the sentence trail off, but the inference was clear.

An expression of hopeless resignation settled over Cordell's features. "Where do you want me to start?"

"Take it from five o'clock the afternoon it happened."

The tortured man wet his lips. "Five o'clock was when my shift went off at the plant. The plant, in case you've forgotten, is the Ames Chemical Company, and I'm a foreman in the Dry Packaging department."

"Save your sarcasm," Kirk said equably.

"Yeah. I changed clothes and punched out around five-fifteen. Juanita had called me about four and said to pick her up at Professor Gilmore's laboratory."

"At what time?"

"No special time. Just when I could get out there. We were going to have dinner and take in a movie. No particular picture; she said we'd pick one out of the paper at dinner."

"Go on."

"Well, it must've been about quarter to six when I got out to the University. I parked in front of the laboratory wing and went in at the main entrance. I walked down the corridor to the Professor's office. His typist was knocking out some letters and there were a couple of students hanging around waiting for him to show up. How about a smoke, Lieutenant?"

Kirk nodded to one of the men behind him and a package of cigarettes was extended to the man under the light. A match was proffered and the young man ignited the white tube, his hands shaking badly.

The Lieutenant crossed his legs the other way, "Let's hear the rest of it, friend."

"What for?" Bitterness tinged Cordell's voice. "You don't believe a word I'm saying."

"Up to now I do."

"Well, I said something or other to Alma—she's the Prof's secretary—and went on through the door to the hall that leads to the private lab. When I got—"

Kirk held up a hand. "Wait a minute. Your busting right in on the Professor like that doesn't sound right. Why not wait in the office for your wife?"

"What for?" Cordell squinted at him in surprise. "He and I get...got along fine. When Juanita first went to work for him he said to drop in at the lab any time, not to wait in the outer office like a freshman or something."

"Go ahead."

"Well..." The young man hesitated. "We're back to the part you *don't* believe, Officer. I can't hardly believe it myself; but so help me, it's gospel. I *saw* it!"

"I'm waiting."

Cordell said doggedly: "The lab door was open a crack. I heard a woman's voice in there, and it wasn't my wife's. It was a voice like—like cracked ice. You know: cold and kind of...well...brittle and—and deadly. That's the only way I can describe it.

"Anyway, I sort of hesitated there, outside the door. I didn't want to go bulling in on something that wasn't none of my business...but on the other hand I figured my wife was in there, else Alma would've said so."

"You hear anything besides this collection of ice cubes?"

The young man's jaw hardened. "I'm giving it the way it happened. You want the rest, or you want to trade wise cracks?"

One of the men behind Kirk lunged forward, "Why, you cheap punk—"

Kirk stopped him with an arm. "I'll handle this, Miller." To Cordell: "I asked you a question. Answer it."

"I heard Professor Gilmore. Only a couple words, then two quick flashes of light lit up the frosted glass door panel. That's when I heard these two thumps like when somebody falls down. I shoved open the door fast...and right then I saw *her!*"

Kirk nodded for no apparent reason and was careful about knocking a quarter inch of ash off his cigar. "Tell me about her."

The young man's hands were shaking again. He sucked at his cigarette and let the smoke come out with his words: "She was clear over on the other side of the lab...standing a good two feet off the floor in the middle of a big blue ball of some kind of—of soft fire. *Blue* fire that sort of *pulsed*—you know. Anyway, there she was: this hell of a good-looking blonde; looking right smack at me, and there was this funny kind of gun in her hand. She aimed it and I ducked just as this dim flash of light came out of it. Something hit me on the side of the head and I...well, I guess I blanked out."

"Then what?"

"Well, like I said yesterday, I suppose I just naturally came out of it. I'm all spread out on the floor with the damndest headache you ever saw. Over by the window is the Prof and"—he wet his lips—"and Juanita. They're dead, Lieutenant; just kind of all piled up over there...dead, their heads busted in and the—the—the—"

He sat there, his mouth working but no sound coming out, his eyes staring straight into the blazing light, the

She was standing a good two feet off the floor in the middle of a glowing bubble that pulsed and wavered around her.

cigarette smouldering, forgotten, between the first two fingers of his left hand.

Almost gently Kirk said: "Let's go back to where you were standing outside the door. You heard this woman talking. What did she say?"

Cordell looked sightlessly down at his hands. "Nothing that made sense. Sounded, near as I can remember, like: 'Twelve times zero'—then some words, or more numbers maybe—I'm not sure—then she said, 'Chained to a two hundred thousand years'—and the Professor said something about his colleges having no idea and he'd warn them—and the blonde said, 'Three in the past five months'—and then something about taking in washing—"

The detective named Miller gave a derisive grunt. "Of all the goddam stories! Kirk, you gonna listen to any—"

Kirk silenced him with a gesture. "Go on, Cordell."

The young man slowly lifted the cigarette to his mouth, dragged heavily on it, then let it fall to the floor. "That's all. That's when the lights started flashing in there and I tried to be a hero."

"Sure you've left nothing out?"

"You've got it all. The truth, like you wanted."

Kirk said patiently, "Give it up, Cordell. You're as sane as the next guy. Give that story to a jury and they'll figure you're trying to make saps out of them—and when a jury gets sore at a defendant, he gets the limit. And in case you didn't know: in this State, the limit for murder is the hot seat!"

The prisoner stared at him woodenly. "You know I didn't kill my wife—or Professor Gilmore. I had no reason to—no motive. There's *got* to be a motive."

The police officer rubbed his chin reflectively. "Uh-hunh. Motive. How long you married, Cordell?"

"Six years."

"Children?"

"No."

"Ames Chemical pay you a good salary?"

"Enough."

"Enough for two to live on?"

"Sure."

"How long did your wife work for Professor Gilmore?"

"Four years next month."

"What was her job?"

"His assistant."

"Pretty big job for a woman, wasn't it?"

"Juanita held two degrees in nuclear physics."

"You mean this atom bomb stuff?"

"That was part of it."

"Gilmore's a big name in that field, I understand," Kirk said.

"Maybe the biggest."

"Kind of young to rate that high, wouldn't you say? He couldn't have been much past forty."

Cordell shrugged. "He was thirty-eight—and a genius. Genius has nothing to do with age, I hear."

"Not married, I understand."

"That's right." A slow frown was forming on Cordell's face.

"How old was your wife?" Kirk asked.

The frown deepened but the young man answered promptly enough. "Juanita was my age. Twenty-nine."

Martin Kirk eyed his cigar casually. "Why," he said, "did you want her to walk out on her job; to give up her career?"

Cordell stiffened. "Who says I did?" he snapped.

"Are you denying it?"

"You're damn well right I'm denying it! What *is* this?"

Kirk was slowly shaking his head almost pityingly. "On at least two occasions friends of you and your wife have heard you say you wished she'd stay home where she belonged and cut out this 'playing around with a mess of test tubes.' Those are your own words, Cordell."

"Every guy," the young man retorted, "who's got a working wife says something like that now and then. It's only natural."

Kirk's jaw hardened. "But every guy's wife doesn't get murdered."

The other looked at him unbelievingly. "Good God," he burst out, "are you saying I killed Juanita because I wanted her to stop working? Of all the—"

"There's, more!" snapped the Homicide man. "When you passed Professor Gilmore's secretary in his outer office yesterday, what did you say to her?"

"'Say to her?'" the prisoner echoed in a dazed way. "I don't know that I... Some kidding remark, I guess. How do you expect me to remember a thing like that?"

"I'll tell you what you said," Kirk said coldly. "It goes like this: 'Hi, Alma. You think the Prof's through making love to my wife?'"

Cordell's head snapped back and his jaw dropped in utter amazement. "*What!* Of all—! You *nuts*? I never said anything like that in my *life*! Who says I said that?"

Without haste Kirk slid a hand into the inner pocket of his coat and brought out two folded sheets of paper which he opened and spread out on his knee.

"Listen to this, friend," he said softly. "'My name is Miss Alma Dakin. I reside at 1142 Monroe Street, and am employed as secretary to Professor Gregory Gilmore. At approximately 5:50 on the afternoon of October 19, Paul Cordell, husband of Mrs. Juanita Cordell, laboratory assistant to Professor Gilmore, passed my desk on his way into the laboratory. I made no effort to stop him, since my employer had previously instructed me to allow Mr. Cordell to go directly to the laboratory at any time without being announced.'" Kirk looked up at the man in the chair opposite him. "Okay so far?"

Paul Cordell nodded numbly.

"'At the time stated above,'" Kirk, continued, reading from the paper, "'Mr. Cordell stopped briefly in front of my desk. He seemed very angry about something. He said, "Hi, Alma. You think the Prof's through making love to my wife?" Before I could say anything, he turned away and walked into the corridor leading to the laboratory. I continued my work until about five minutes later when Mr.

Cordell came running back into the office and told me to call the police, that Professor Gilmore and Mrs. Cordell had been murdered.

"'Since there is an automatic closer on the corridor door, I did not see Mr. Cordell enter the laboratory itself. I do know, however, that Professor Gilmore and Mrs. Cordell were alone in the laboratory less than ten minutes before Mr. Cordell arrived, as I had just left them alone there after taking some dictation from my employer. Since I went directly to my desk, and since there is no entrance to the laboratory other than through my office, I can state with certainty that Mr. Cordell was the only person to enter the laboratory between 5:00 that afternoon and 5:55 when Mr. Cordell came out of the laboratory and told me of the murders.

"'I hereby depose that this is a true and honest statement, to the best of my knowledge, that it was given freely on my part, and that I have read it before affixing my signature to its pages. Signed: Alma K. Dakin.'"

There was an almost ominous crackle to the document as Lieutenant Kirk folded it and returned it to his pocket. Paul Cordell appeared utterly stunned by what he had heard and his once stiffly squared shoulders were slumped like those of an old man.

"I don't have to tell you," Kirk said, "that the only window in that laboratory is both permanently sealed and heavily barred. No one but you could have murdered those two people. You say you saw them killed by some kind of a gun. Yet a qualified physician states both deaths were caused by a terrific blow from a blunt instrument. We found a lot of things around the lab you could have used to do the job—but nothing at all of anything like a projectile fired from a gun."

The prisoner obviously wasn't listening. "B—but she— she lied!" he stammered wildly. "All I said to Alma Dakin was a couple of words—three or four at the most—about not working too hard. Why should she put me on a spot like that? I just—don't—get—it! Why should she go out of her way to make trouble..." Dawning suspicion replaced his bewilderment. "I get it! You cops put her up to this; that's it! You need a fall guy and I'm elec—"

"Listen to me, Cordell," Kirk cut in impatiently. "You knew, or thought you knew, your wife was having an affair with Professor Gilmore. You tried to break it up, to get her to leave her job. She wasn't having any of that; and the more she refused, the sorer you got. Yesterday you walked in on them unannounced, found them in each other's arms, and knocked them both off in a jealous rage. When you cooled down enough to see what you'd done, you invented this wild yarn about a blonde in a ball of fire, hoping to get off on an insanity plea."

"I want a lawyer!" Cordell shouted.

Kirk ignored the demand. "You're going back to your cell for a couple hours, buster. Think this over. When you're ready to tell it right, I want it in the form of a witnessed statement, on paper. If you do that, if you co-operate with the authorities, you can probably get off with a fairly light sentence, maybe even an outright acquittal, on the old 'unwritten law' plea. I don't make any promises. Gilmore was a prominent man and a valuable one; that might influence a jury against you. But it's the only chance you've got—and I'm telling you, by God, to take it!"

Cordell was standing now, his face working. "Sure; I get it! All you're after is a confession. What do you care if it's a flock of lies? My wife wouldn't even *look* at another man, and not you or anybody else is going to make me say different. That blonde killed them, I tell you—and I'll tell a jury the same thing! They'll believe me; they're not a bunch of lousy framing cops! You'll find out who's—"

Lieutenant Martin Kirk wearily ground out his cigar against the chair rung. "All right, boys. Take him back upstairs."

CHAPTER TWO

It was a gray chill day late in November, and by 4:30 that afternoon the ceiling lights were on. Chenowich, the young plain-clothes man recently transferred to Homicide from Robbery Detail, stopped at Martin Kirk's cubbyhole and slid an evening paper across the battered brown linoleum top of the Lieutenant's desk.

"This oughta interest you," he said, jabbing a chewed thumbnail at an item under a two-column head half-way down the left side of page one.

CORDELL DRAWS DEATH NOD

Killer of Wife and Atom Wizard To Face Chair in January

Paul Cordell, 29, was today doomed by Criminal Court Justice Edwin P. Reed to death by electrocution the morning of January 11, for the murders of his wife, Juanita, 29, and her employer, world-famous nuclear scientist Gregory Gilmore.

A jury last week found Cordell guilty of the brutal slayings despite his testimony that it was a mysterious blonde woman, floating in a "ball of blue fire," who had blasted the victims with a "ray gun" on that October afternoon.

Ignoring the "girl from Mars" angle, alienists for the prosecution pronounced the handsome defendant sane, and his attorneys were powerless to offset the damage.

The final blow to Cordell's hopes for acquittal, however, was administered by the State's key witness, Alma Dakin, Gilmore's former secretary. For more than three hours she underwent one of the most grilling cross-examinations in local courtroom...

Kirk shoved the paper aside. "What could he expect when he wouldn't even listen to his own lawyers? They'll appeal—they have to—but it'll be a waste of time."

He leaned back in the creaking swivel chair and began to unwrap the cellophane from a cigar. "In a way," he said thoughtfully, "I hate to see that kid end up in the fireless cooker. In this business you get so you can recognize an act when you see one, and I'd swear Cordell wasn't lying about that blonde and her blue fire. At least he thought he wasn't."

Chenowich yawned. "I say he was nuts then and he's nuts now. What do them bug doctors know? I never seen one yet could count his own fingers."

The telephone on Martin Kirk's desk rang while he was lighting his cigar. He tossed the match on the floor to join a dozen others, and picked up the receiver. "Homicide; Lieutenant Kirk speaking."

It was the patrolman in the outer office. "Woman out here wants to see you, Lieutenant. Asked for you personally."

"What about?"

"She won't say. All I get is it's important and she talks to you or nobody."

"What's her name?"

"No, sir. Not even that. Want me to get rid of her?"

Kirk eyed the mound of paper work on his desk and sighed. "Probably a taxpayer. All right; send her back here."

A moment later the patrolman loomed up outside the cubbyhole door, the woman in tow. Lieutenant Kirk remained seated, nodded briskly toward the empty chair alongside his desk. "Please sit down, madam. You wanted to see me?"

"You are Mr. Kirk?" A warm voice, almost on the husky side.

"Lieutenant Kirk."

"Of course. I *am* sorry."

While she was being graceful about getting into the chair, Kirk stared at her openly. She was worth staring at. She was tall for a woman and missed being voluptuous by exactly the right margin. Her face was more lovely than beautiful, chiefly because of large eyes so blue they were almost purple. Her skin was flawless, her blonde hair worn in a medium bob fluffed out, and her smooth fitting tobacco brown suit must have been bought by appointment. She looked to be in her mid-twenties and was probably thirty.

Her expression was solemn and her smile fleeting, as was becoming to anyone calling on a Homicide Bureau. She placed on a corner of Kirk's desk an alligator bag that matched her shoes and tucked pale yellow gloves the color of her blouse under the bag's strap. Her slim fingers, ringless, moved competently and without haste.

"I am Naia North, Lieutenant Kirk."

"What's on your mind, Miss North?"

She regarded him gravely, seeing gray-blue eyes that never quite lost their chill, a thin nose bent slightly to the left from an encounter with a drunken longshoreman years before, the lean lines of a solid jaw, the dark hair that was beginning to thin out above the temples after thirty-five years. Even those who love him, she thought, must fear this man a little.

Martin Kirk felt his cheeks flush under the frank appraisal of those purple eyes. "You asked for me by name, Miss North. Why?"

"Aren't you the officer who arrested the young man who today was sentenced to die?"

Only years of practise at letting nothing openly surprise him kept Kirk's jaw from dropping. "...You mean Cordell?"

"Yes."

"I'm the one. What about it? What've you got to do with Paul Cordell?"

Naia North said quietly, "A great deal, I'm afraid. You see, I'm the woman who doesn't exist; the one the newspapers call 'the girl from Mars.'"

It was what he had expected from her first question about the case. Any murder hitting the headlines brought at least one psycho out of the woodwork, driven by some deep-seated sense of guilt into making a phony confession. Those who were harmless were eased aside; the violent got detained for observation.

But Naia North showed none of the signs of the twisted mind. She was coherent, attractive and obviously there was money somewhere in her vicinity. While the last two items could have been true of a raving maniac, Kirk was human enough to be swayed by them.

"I'm afraid," he said, "you've come to the wrong man about this, Miss North." His smile was frank and winning enough to startle her. "The case is out of my hands; has been since the District Attorney's office took over. Why don't you take it up with them?"

Her short laugh was openly cynical. "I tried to, the day the trial ended. I got as far as a fourth assistant, who told me the case was closed, that new and conclusive evidence would be necessary to reopen it, and would I excuse him as he had a golf date. When I said I could give him new evidence, he looked at his watch and wanted me to write a letter. So I wrote one and his secretary promised to hand it to him personally. I'm still waiting for an answer."

"These things take time, Miss North. If I were you I'd—"

"I even tried to see Judge Reed. I got as far as his bailiff. If I'd state my business in writing...I did; that's the last I've heard from Judge Reed *or* bailiff."

Kirk picked up his cigar from the edge of the desk and tapped the ash onto the floor. "Shall I," he said, his lips quirking, "ask you to write *me* a letter?"

Naia North failed to respond to the light touch. "I'm through filling wastebaskets," she said flatly. "Either you do something about this or the newspapers get the entire story. Not that I'll enjoy being a public spectacle, but at least they'll give me some action."

"What do you want done?"

She put both elbows on the desk top and bent toward him. He caught the faint odor of bath salts rising from under the rounded neckline of her blouse. "That man must go free, Lieutenant. He didn't kill his wife—*or* Gregory Gilmore."

"Who did?"

She looked straight into his eyes. "I did."

"Why?"

Slowly she straightened and leaned back in the chair, her gaze shifting to a point beyond his left shoulder. "Nothing you haven't heard before," she said tonelessly.

"We met several months ago and fell in love. I let him make the rules...and after a while he got tired of playing. I didn't—and I wanted him back. For weeks he avoided me."

"So you decided to kill him."

She seemed genuinely astonished at the remark. "Certainly not! But when I saw him take this woman—this assistant of his, or whatever she was—into his arms. I suppose I went a little crazy."

"Now," Kirk said, "we're getting down to cases. You know the evidence given at the trial—particularly that given by Gilmore's secretary?"

"Of course."

"Then you know this Dakin woman was in the laboratory until a few minutes before Cordell showed up. You know that nobody could have gone into that laboratory without her seeing them. You know that Alma Dakin testified that there were only two people in there: Gilmore and Juanita Cordell. So, Miss North, how did you get in there after Alma Dakin left and before Paul Cordell arrived?"

"But I didn't."

The Lieutenant's air of triumph sagged under a sudden frown. "What do you mean you didn't?"

"I didn't enter the laboratory after Greg's secretary left it. *I was there all along.*"

Kirk's head came up sharply. "You *what?*"

"I was there all the time," the girl repeated. "Since noon, to be exact. I planned it that way. I knew everybody would be out to lunch between twelve and one, so I went to the laboratory with the intention of facing Greg there on his return. When I heard him and Mrs. Cordell coming along the corridor, I sort of lost my nerve and hid in a coat closet."

Martin Kirk had completely dropped his air of good-humored patience by this time. "You telling me you were hiding in there for almost five hours without them knowing it?"

Naia North shrugged her shoulders. "They had no reason to look in the closet. I'll admit I hadn't intended to—to spy on Greg. But I kept waiting for him to say or do something that would prove or disprove he was in love with Juanita Cordell, and not until his secretary left and he was alone with her did I discover what was between them. I must have come out of that dark hole like a tiger, Lieutenant. They jumped apart and two people never looked guiltier. He said something particularly nasty to me and I grabbed up a short length of shiny metal from the workbench and hit him across the side of the head before he knew what was happening. He fell down and the Cordell woman opened her mouth to scream and—and I hit her too."

She paused as though to permit Kirk to comment. "Go on," he said hoarsely.

"There's not much left," the girl said. "I was standing there still holding that piece of metal when the door crashed open and the dead woman's husband ran in. He started to lunge across the room at me and I threw the thing I was holding at him. It struck him and he fell down. My only thought was to hide, for I realized I couldn't go out through the outer office, and the only window was barred. So I hid in that closet again.

"It was only a few minutes before Paul Cordell regained consciousness. He staggered out of the room and down the hall and I could hear a lot of excited talk and Greg's secretary calling the police. Then I didn't hear anything at all for a moment, so I came out of the closet and looked down the hall. The office door was closed, but it seemed so quiet in there that I tiptoed quickly to the inner door, opened it a crack and peered through. The office was deserted; evidently Cordell and Miss Dakin had gone out to direct the police when they showed up.

"When I saw there was no one in the main hall of the building itself, I simply walked out and left by another exit. No one I passed even noticed me."

For a long time after Naia North had finished speaking, Martin Kirk sat as though carved from stone, staring blindly into space. She knew he was thinking furiously, weighing the plausibility of what he had heard, trying to arrive at some method of corroborating it in a way that would stand up in a court of law.

"Miss North."

She came out of a reverie with a start, to find the Lieutenant's eyes boring into hers. "This shiny hunk of metal you used: where is it now?"

"I'm sure I wouldn't know. Probably some place in the laboratory, unless somebody took it away. I do seem to remember picking it up and tossing it back with several others like it on the bench."

"Then it's still there," he said slowly. "Judge Reed ordered the room sealed up until after the trial. And then there's the closet... Were you wearing gloves that afternoon, Miss North?"

She said, "No. You're thinking of fingerprints?"

"If you're telling the truth," he said, "there's almost certain to be some of your prints on the inside of that closet door—maybe even on that length of metal, if we can find it."

She said almost carelessly: "That's all you'd need to clear Paul Cordell, isn't it?"

"It would certainly help." He swung around in the chair, scooped up the telephone and gave a series of rapid-fire orders, then dropped the instrument on its cradle and turned back to where she sat watching him curiously.

He said, "A few things I still don't get. Like this business of your standing two feet off the floor in a ball of blue light. And the flashes of light just before Cordell heard his wife and Gilmore fall to the floor. Even the snatches of conversation he caught while still in the hall. He couldn't have dreamed all that stuff up—at least not without *some* basis."

She had opened her bag and taken out a cigarette. Kirk ignited one of his kitchen matches and she bent her head for a light. He could see the flawless curve of one cheek and the smooth cap of blonde hair, and he resisted the urge to pass a hand lightly across both. Something was stirring inside the Lieutenant—something that had long been absent. And, he reflected wryly, all because of a girl who had just finished confessing to two particularly unpleasant murders.

Naia North raised her head and their eyes met—met and held. Her lips parted slightly as she caught the unmistakable message in those gray-blue depths…

The moment passed, the spell was broken and she leaned back in the chair and laughed a little shakily. "I read about those statements of his in the papers, Lieutenant. I think perhaps I can at least partially explain them. As I remember it, there were several Bunsen burners lighted on the laboratory bench near that window. They give off a blue flame, you know, and I must have been standing near them when Paul Cordell came charging in. In his confused frame of mind, he may have pictured me as being in a ball of flame."

"Sounds possible," the man admitted, frowning. "What about those flashes of light?"

"You've got me there. Unless they were reflections of sunlight through the window—from the windshield of a passing car, perhaps."

"And the things he heard you and Gilmore saying?"

She shook her head regretfully.

"There I'm simply in the dark, I don't see how he could have twisted what little we said into the utterly fantastic nonsense he claims to have heard."

Kirk rubbed a hand slowly along the side of his neck, still frowning. "He *could* have confused that length of metal in your hand as a gun… Well—" his shoulders lifted in the ghost of a shrug—"it all seems to add up. Except one thing: Cordell had been tried and convicted, leaving you in the clear. Why come down here voluntarily and stick your lovely head in a noose?"

The girl smiled faintly. "'Lovely head, Lieutenant?'"

Kirk flushed to the eyebrows. "That slipped out... Why the confession?"

She said soberly: "I was so sure they'd let him off. When you *know* someone's innocent you can't realize that others won't know it too, I suppose. But when I learned he'd been found guilty and actually condemned to die...well, I know it sounds noble and all that but I couldn't let him go to his death for something I'd done. Surely such a thing has happened before in your experience, Lieutenant."

He watched as she drew smoke from the cigarette deeply into her lungs and let it flow out in twin streamers from her nostrils. Only rich men, he thought, could afford a woman like this, and somehow it made him resentful. What right did she have to walk in here and flaunt a body like that in his face? She went with mink stoles and cabin cruisers and cocktails at the Sherry-Netherland, and her shoe bill would exceed his yearly salary. She would be competent and more than a little cynical and not too concerned with morals or the lack of them. That kind of woman could kill—and would kill, on the spur of the moment and if the provocation was strong enough.

"Well, Lieutenant?" She said it lightly, almost with disinterest.

Then Kirk was all right again, and he was looking at a woman who had just confessed to murder.

"You heard the phone call I made a moment ago, Miss North. Two men from the Crime Lab are already on their way to the University. If they find your fingerprints inside that closet, if they can turn up *anything* to prove you've been in Gregory Gilmore's laboratory, then you and that evidence and your confession get turned over to the D. A. and Paul Cordell will be on his way to freedom."

"And if those men don't find anything?"

"Then," he told her rudely, "you're just another crackpot and I'm tossing you *and* your phony confession out of here."

They found the fingerprints: several perfect ones on the inner door of the laboratory coat closet. But even more conclusive was their discovery of a short length of polished metal pipe among the dismantled parts of a Clayton centrifuge. At one end of the pipe were the imprints of four fingertips—at the other a microscopic trace of human blood.

"We had no business missing it the first time, Lieutenant," the Crime Laboratory technician told Kirk ruefully. "I'd a sworn we pulled that place apart last month. But this time we got the murder weapon and we got the prints—and those prints match the ones we took off that blonde. Hey, how about that, Lieutenant? I thought this Cordell guy did that job?"

Slowly Kirk replaced the receiver and eyed Naia North across the desk from him. "Looks like you're elected," he said somberly. "I'm telling you straight: the D. A. isn't going to like this at all—not even any part of it."

Her brow wrinkled. "I'm afraid I don't understand. Doesn't he want murder cases solved?"

Kirk smiled crookedly. "You're forgetting this case *was* solved—over a month ago. You any idea what it can mean to a politician to have to admit publicly that he's made a mistake? Especially a mistake that's going to get all the publicity this one's bound to? 'District attorney railroads innocent man!' 'Tragic miscarriage of justice averted only by chance!' Stuffy editorials in the opposition press about incompetence in high offices and how the voters must keep out anybody who goes around executing the innocent and helpless. Looks like Arthur Kahler Troy is going to be a mighty unpopular man around these parts—and election less than five months away!"

He glanced up at the office clock. It was nearly nine o'clock in the evening, and both of them were showing signs of wear. Kirk left his chair and went over to the water cooler, drank two cupfuls and brought one back to the girl. She thanked him with a wan smile and gulped down the contents.

He took the empty paper container and crumpled it slowly. "Might as well get hold of him," he muttered. "It's going to be mighty damned rough, sister. You sure you want to go through with it?"

She lifted an eyebrow at him. "That's a peculiar question for a homicide officer to ask, isn't it?"

"I suppose so." His eyes shifted to the phone on his desk, stayed there for a long moment. Then he shrugged hugely and picked up the receiver...

It was well after two in the morning before Martin Kirk reached his apartment. He showered and got into a fresh pair of pajamas and went into the small, sparsely furnished living room. He moved slowly and with no spring in his step, and the set of his features was harsh and strained in the soft light from the floor lamp.

Troy had been even more difficult than he'd feared. What had begun as plain irritability at being disturbed, had passed by successive stages to amused disbelief, open anger and finally reluctant conviction that Paul Cordell was innocent of the crimes for which he had been sentenced to die.

A male stenographer from his staff was called in and Naia North dictated a complete statement which she signed. Troy questioned her for nearly two hours, getting in every possible angle of her private life as well as minute details of her actions on the day of the murders. Kirk had not been present during that part of the night, but he figured it wouldn't be much different from what he'd heard many times before.

He mixed himself a drink, and was surprised to discover that his hands were shaking noticeably. Well, why not? A day like the one he'd just been through would put the shakes in Grant's Tomb. Even as he made the excuse, he knew it wasn't the real reason. There had been cases that had kept him on his feet for as much as forty-eight hours—cases where men had pointed guns at him and pulled the triggers—and the shakes never came.

No, it was the girl. Naia North. Naia—a strange name. But no stranger than the girl herself. Now how about that? Why should he think her strange? Because she'd taken a life or two? Hell, lots of people did that and no one called them strange. Criminal or unmoral or greedy or angry, yes. But not strange. She looked like other women—only a lot better. She dressed like them, walked like them, talked like them. So why strange?

Because she *was* strange. Nothing you could put your finger on made her that way, but that's the way she was.

He threw his cigar savagely into the fireplace. He went over and made another drink and poured it down fast and another one after it, right on its heels. Then he went to bed. Tomorrow—today, rather—was a work day and work days were tough days and he needed his rest.

He didn't get much of it, though. The phone woke him a few minutes after seven o'clock. It was Arthur Kahler Troy at the other end and the D. A. was too angry to be coherent.

It seemed Naia North had disappeared from her locked cell during the night.

CHAPTER THREE

"I don't give a triple-distilled damn *what* you say!" Troy snarled. "Nobody's got enough money to make that kind of payoff. Five men, Lieutenant—five men and five locked doors stood between that girl and the street. And you sit there and try to tell me somebody bought all *five* of 'em off!"

"Then," Kirk said heatedly, "what's *your* explanation?"

It had been going on this way for over an hour. The morning sun came in weakly at the window behind Troy's huge polished mahogany desk, picking up random reflections from the collection of expensive gadgets littering the glass top.

Troy began to wear another path in the moss-colored broadloom carpeting. He was big and broad and getting puffy around the middle, like a one-time halfback going to seed. His round, heavy-featured face was even more florid than usual, and his heavy growth of reddish-blond hair needed a comb.

Martin Kirk pushed himself deeper into the depths of a brown leather chair and watched the D. A. through brooding eyes. He wanted a cigar but it was too early in the morning for that kind of indulgence. You needed a good breakfast and a couple cups of coffee before—

"I don't explain it," Troy said in quieter tones. He was standing by the window now, staring down into the boulevard passing that side of the Criminal Courts Building. "It's one of those things that make me think my sainted mother wasn't so wrong when she used to tell about elves and gnomes and leprechauns and fairies and—"

Kirk made a sound deep in his throat, "Naia North was a hell of a long way from being a leprechaun. Somebody wanted her out of here for some reason—and they got her out. I want to know who took her out, why she was taken, and where she is now. And I'm going to find out the answers to all three if I have to turn this town on its ear."

"Go ahead," Troy said. "Hop right to it and I wish you luck. Only leave me and my people out of it."

"Seems to me you're mighty damned anxious *to* be left out."

Arthur Kahler Troy turned on his heel and strode toward the Lieutenant until he was towering over him. "Just what," he said between his teeth, "do you mean by *that* crack?"

"Figure it out for yourself," Kirk snapped. "And I'm sure you can."

Troy reared back as though the police officer had pulled a gun on him. "Why—why you—I'll have you busted for making a dirty insinu—"

"You couldn't bust a daisy chain at the police department," Kirk growled. "The Commissioner hates your guts and you know that as well as I do. Now let's cut out all this hokey-pokey and pick up a few loose ends. The first thing: what about Paul Cordell?"

All the wide-eyed fury seemed to go out of Troy's face like water down the bathtub drain. He turned away and walked slowly back to his desk chair and sat down.

He said, "What about Cordell," in a soft voice.

"The morning paper," Kirk said, "reports he was taken up to Hillcrest last night. The warden out there's probably got him in Death Row already."

"Uh-hunh."

"Well, let's get him out of there. With the evidence we've got, plus Naia North's sworn statement, Judge Reed will have to bring him back down here and release him—at least on bail until we can find the girl. The man's innocent, Mr. D. A.; have you forgotten?"

"Yes."

"Yes? Yes, what?"

"I've forgotten he's innocent," Troy said quietly. "Matter of fact, he's guilty as hell."

The Lieutenant half rose from his chair. "Now wait a minute! You heard that girl's story and you've got the evidence I turned over to you right here in this office last night. What more—"

"I'll tell you what more," Troy snapped. "That girl was a fraud, her story was a downright lie and that evidence was faked. Let me tell you something else, Mister: within five minutes after the guard downstairs reported your girl friend missing, I had five squads of my men out running down the personal information she gave me a few hours before. And you know what they found out? *Every bit of what she told me was false!* Hear that? False! It took my men about one hour to prove as much, for the simple reason that not one lead panned out. Not one! And you know what *I* think?"

Martin Kirk opened his mouth but nothing came out but a strangled croak.

"I think you and this dame worked out the whole thing between the two of you to save Cordell's neck. Who could do a better job of faking evidence than a crooked cop? What's more, you might have gotten away with it, too—only it suddenly dawned on the girl that she was getting in too deep."

"And so," Kirk cut in hotly, "she calmly walked through five locked sets of iron bars and went back to Mars!"

He stood up and crossed to the desk and leaned down with his palms in the center of the brown blotter. "You won't get away with it, Troy. You didn't want any part of this new development from the minute I called you on the phone last night. You knew it could show you and your whole organization up as a bunch of bunglers and incompetents. So you got rid of the girl, thinking that without her the truth of those murders would never get out to the voters.

"Well, it won't work, Fatso! The evidence I dug up is strong enough to reopen the case *without* Naia. All I have to do is put that evidence in front of Judge Reed, and—"

Troy was smiling wolfishly. "*What* evidence, Lieutenant?"

Kirk stiffened. "You know damned well what evidence. It's in your files right now: Naia North's statement, the strips of paneling from that coat closet, the murder weapon. I turned the whole works over to you."

The D. A. was shaking his head. "We don't keep worthless junk around here, my boy. The Cordell case is closed; the guilty man is awaiting execution. Sure, you run along and tell the Judge all about it. Tell the newspapers, tell Cordell's defense attorneys, tell the world for all I care. See who'll touch it without something more concrete than your highly imaginative daydreams. For all you can prove, the girl might have confessed the whole thing was a hoax and we tossed her out of here last night...

"I'm a busy man, Lieutenant. Good morning—good luck—and kindly close the door on your way out."

CHAPTER FOUR

Lieutenant Martin Kirk shoved the pile of mimeographed pages aside. Three hours spent in going through the complete transcript of the Cordell trial and nothing to show for it but stiff muscles and an aching head.

Give it up, a small voice in the back of his mind urged. You haven't got a leg to stand on as far as getting any action out of the authorities. Troy and his gang put the fear of God in that purple-eyed dame and shipped her out of the State. You lose, brother—and so does that poor devil up on Death's Row.

He drummed his fingers over and over on the arm of his chair and listened to the everyday sounds of a normal day at the Homicide Bureau. A new day, a new set of problems, and why knock yourself out over something that doesn't concern you? Thing to do was go down to the corner tavern and have a couple of fast ones and watch an old movie on television. Yes sir, that's exactly what he'd do!

He went back to the mimeographed pages.

For the fourth time he read through Cordell's testimony of what had happened that October afternoon. And it was there that he came across the first possible break in the stone wall.

Once more Martin Kirk went over the few lines, although by this time he could have come close to reciting them from memory. It was an excerpt from Arthur Kahler Troy's cross-examination of the defendant after Cordell's counsel, in a last desperate effort to swing the tide of a losing battle, had placed him on the stand.

Q: (by Troy): Now, Mr. Cordell, I direct your attention to the point in your testimony at which you first entered Professor Gilmore's outer office. At what time was this?

A: At about 5:45 p.m.

Q: Who was in the office at that time?

A: Alma Dakin, the Professor's secretary. And a couple of students—although they were at the other end of the room and I didn't pay much attention to them.

Q: But you did pay attention, as you call it, to Miss Dakin?

A: Well, I spoke to her, if that's what you mean.

Q: That's exactly what I mean, Mr. Cordell. And what was it you said to her?

A: Something about it was too late in the day to be working so hard.

Q: That was all?

A: Yes, sir.

Q: Remember, Mr. Cordell, you're under oath. Now I ask you again: Was that all you said to her at that time?

A: Yes, sir.

Q: It isn't possible you've forgotten some additional remark? Think carefully, please.

A: No, sir. That's all I said. I swear it.

Q: Very well. Now how well do you know Miss Dakin?

A: Just to speak to.

Q: Have you ever seen her outside Professor Gilmore's office?

A: No, sir.

Q: Ever ask her for a date?

A: No, sir.

Q: Did you ever have an argument with her? A discussion of any kind that may have become a bit heated?

A: No, sir.

Q: Then to your knowledge she'd have no reason to dislike you?

A: No, sir.

Q: Very good. Now, Mr. Cordell, I want to read to you an excerpt from the testimony given by Miss Dakin in this court. "Mr. Cordell was looking very angry when he came in. He came up to me and bent down over the desk and said so low I could hardly hear him: 'Hi, Alma. You think the Prof's through making love to my wife?'" I now ask you, Paul Cordell, isn't that what you said to Alma Dakin? Not that she was working too hard, or whatever it was you claimed to have said.

A: No, sir. I didn't say anything like she said I did. I wouldn't insult my wife by saying such a thing to a third—

Q: Just answer the questions, Mr. Cordell. Then you contend that Miss Dakin deliberately lied in her testimony.

A: She was mistaken.

Q: Oh, come now! Miss Dakin is an intelligent girl; she couldn't misunderstand or twist your words to that extent. Now could she?

A: Then she lied. I never said anything like that.

Q: What reason would she have for lying, Mr. Cordell? By your own statement she hardly knew you, always greeted you pleasantly on the times you came to the office, never got into any arguments with you, and never saw you outside the office. She had worked for Professor Gilmore for five or six months, has excellent references, and is well liked by her friends. Yet you're asking us to believe that she coldly and deliberately lied to get you into trouble. Is that true?

A: All I know is she lied.

The break was there all right, Kirk thought grimly. For if Cordell was innocent, then he had told the truth during the trial. And if he had told the truth about his remark to Alma Dakin, then, automatically, Alma Dakin's testimony was untrue.

Kirk ran his fingers through his hair in a gesture of bafflement. What possible reason could Gilmore's secretary have for going out of her way to lie about Cordell's remark? Was it because she was so certain he had killed her employer that she wanted to make sure he would be punished?

Or was it because she wanted to shield the real killer? Maybe she was a friend of Naia North's and had known the blonde girl was in Gilmore's laboratory all along. She might even have deliberately steered everyone out of her office after Cordell discovered the bodies, making it possible for Naia to slip out unseen.

It was a slender lead, but the only one large enough to get even a fingernail grip on. He drew the phone over in front of him and began a series of calls designated to give him more information about Alma Dakin.

A call to the University took him through a couple of secretaries before he reached the right person. Her name was Miss Slife, personnel director of all non-teaching employees. Miss Dakin? Why, of course! A lovely girl and very dependable. She had come to the University in search of a position only a day or two before Miss Collins, Professor Gilmore's previous secretary, had resigned. Since Miss Dakin's references showed that she had worked for a short time as secretary to Dr. Karney, one of the co-discoverers of the atom bomb (according to Miss Slife), she had been engaged to take Miss Collins' place. Professor Gilmore, poor man, had been very pleased with the change and everybody was happy: Miss Collins at inheriting a vary large sum of money from a relative she'd never even heard of, Miss Dakin at being able to get such a nice position, and *dear* Professor Gilmore at finding such a satisfactory replacement.

When Miss Slife had run down, Kirk said, "This Dr. Karney. Why did Miss Dakin leave him?"

The woman at the other end of the wire seemed astonished by Kirk's ignorance. "Why, I assumed *everybody* knew about Dr. Karney. He died of a heart attack about eight months ago."

"*What!*"

"Goodness, there's no need to shout, Mr. Kirk. He was connected with Clement University, out in California, and suffered a stroke of some kind while at work."

Kirk thanked her dazedly and broke the connection. This, he told himself, is too much a coincidence to *be* a coincidence! Two prominent nuclear scientists dying suddenly within seven months of each other at opposite ends of the country—and both of them with the same secretary at the time of their deaths!

A sudden thought sent him leafing rapidly through the trial transcript to the place where Paul Cordell had told of the disjointed phrases he claimed to have heard before he pushed into Professor Gilmore's laboratory. The words he sought seemed to stand out in letters of fire: "...three in the past five months..."

Again he caught up the telephone receiver, aware that his heart was pounding with excitement, and dialed a number... "*Bulletin?* Hello; let me talk to Jerry Furness... Jerry, this is Martin Kirk at Homicide. Look, do something for me. I want to find out how many top nuclear fission boys have died in the past four or five months... No, no; nothing like that. Some of the boys down here were having an argument about... Sure; I'll hold on."

He propped the receiver between his ear and shoulder and groped for a cigar. In the office beyond the partition of his cubbyhole a woman was sobbing. Chenowich went past his open door whistling a radio commercial.

The receiver against his ear began to vibrate. "Yeah, Jerry... Four of 'em, hey? Let's have their names." He picked up a pencil and took down the information. "*Uh-hunh!* Three heart attacks and one murder. Check... You mean *all* of them? Tough life, I guess... Yeah, sure. Anytime. So long."

He replaced the receiver with slow care and leaned back to study the list of names. Not counting the last name—Gilmore's—three world-renowned men in the field of nuclear physics had dropped dead from heart failure within the designated span of months.

Coincidence? Maybe. But he was in no mood for coincidences. If the deaths of these four scientists was the result of some sinister plan, who was responsible? Some foreign power, concerned about this country's growing mastery of nuclear fission? Was it his duty to notify the FBI of his findings and let them take over from here?

He shook his head. Too early for anything like that. He needed more evidence—evidence not to be explained away as coincidence.

Once more Lieutenant Martin Kirk went back to analyzing the broken phrases Cordell had picked up while eavesdropping that October afternoon. *Twelve times zero* made no sense at all...unless it could be the combination of a safe...? Hardly possible; no combination he'd ever heard of would read that way. The next one, then...*chained to two hundred thousand years...* Another blank; could mean anything or nothing. Next: *A: ...sounded like the Professor said something like his colleges had no idea and he'd see they were warned right away.*

Kirk bit thoughtfully down on a corner of his lip. Gilmore didn't own any colleges and how do you go about warning one? Maybe the word was *college*, meaning the one where he had his laboratory. But actually it wasn't a college at all; it was a university. Not much difference to the man in the street, but to the Professor... Wait a minute! Not *colleges!* *Colleagues!* It was his colleagues Gilmore had promised to warn. And the word meant men and women in the same line of work as the Professor—nuclear physics. Things, Kirk told himself with elation, were looking up!

The business about "three in the past five months" was next, but he felt sure of what that had meant. But the last of the quotations went nowhere at all.

"Something about *taking in washing*—" Under less tragic circumstances, a nonsense line. But Cordell hadn't actually heard the words clearly enough to quote them with authority. That could mean he had heard words that sounded *like* "taking in washing."

Taking, baking, making, slaking, raking—the list seemed endless. "Washing" could have been the first two syllables of Washington—and Washington would be the place where the Atomic Energy Commission hung out.

Still too hazy. He leaned back and put his feet up and attacked the three mysterious words from every conceivable angle. No dice.

Sight of the ambling figure of Patrolman Chenowich passing the office door caught his eye, reminding him that two heads were often better than one. "Hey, Frank."

Chenowich came in. "Yeah, Lieutenant. Somethin' doin'?"

"I'm trying to figure out a little problem," Kirk explained carelessly. "Let's say you hear a guy talking in the next room. You can't really make out the words he's saying, but right in the middle of his mumbling you hear what sounds like 'taking in washing.' Now you know that can't be right, so you try to think out what he actually *did* say..."

It was obvious Chenowich had fallen off on the first curve, so completely off that Kirk didn't bother finishing what was much too involved to begin with. The patrolman was staring at him in monstrous perplexity.

"Jeez, Lieutenant. I don't get it. 'Less the guy's goin' to open up one of these here laundries. That way he'd be takin' in washin'. But I don't know what else—"

Kirk's feet hit the floor with a solid thump and he grabbed Chenowich's wrist with fingers that bit in like steel. "Say that again!" he shouted. "Say it just that way!"

The patrolman recoiled in alarm. "What's got into you, Lieutenant? Say *what?*"

"Taking in washing!"

"Takin' in washin'? What for?"

Kirk's grin threatened to split his face, "The same words," he said, "but you say them different. Only your way's the right way! Thanks, pal. Now get out of here!"

Chenowich went. His mouth was still open and his expression still troubled, but he went.

The last of the killer's cryptic remarks was now clear. For Kirk realized that "takin'" rhymed with words you'd never associate with "taking." "Bacon", for instance—or "Dakin"! Alma Dakin, former secretary to two widely separated, and now dead, nuclear scientists. Her name had been mentioned by the slayer of Professor Gilmore only seconds before she had clubbed the savant to death.

But now that "taking" had come out "Dakin"—what did the rest of the phrase mean? *Dakin in washing* made no sense. What sounded like *washing?* Washing; washing...*watching?* It was close; in fact nothing he could think of came closer.

All right. *Dakin in watching;* no. *Dakin is watching*—that made sense. But Alma Dakin hadn't been watching anything at the time of the killing; she, according to Cordell, was at her desk in the outer office. That would leave *Dakin was watching* as the right combination. Watching for the right opportunity for murder!

What did it mean? Well, assuming from her past record that Alma Dakin was mixed up in the deaths of two prominent men of science, it argued that she and Naia North were accomplices in a scheme to rid America of her nuclear fission experts. The nice smooth story of killing Gilmore because of unrequited love was probably as much a lie as the personal information Naia North had given Arthur Kahler Troy.

The North girl had confessed to murdering Gilmore and Juanita Cordell. As a confessed killer she must be taken into custody and booked on suspicion of homicide. Taking her was Martin Kirk's job—and it seemed he had a contact that would lead him to her. Namely Alma Dakin.

Lieutenant Kirk grabbed his hat and went out the door.

CHAPTER FIVE

The address for Alma Dakin turned out to be a small three-story walk-up apartment building on a quiet residential street near the outskirts of town. At two in the afternoon hardly anyone was visible on the sidewalks and only an occasional automobile passed.

Kirk parked his car half a block further on down and got out into the chill November air. He entered the building foyer and looked at the name plates above the twin rows of buttons. The one for Alma Dakin told him the number of her apartment was 3C.

He pushed the button several times but without response. The foyer was very quiet at this time of day, and he could hear the faint rasp of her bell through the speaking tube.

Kirk was on the point of shifting his thumb to the button marked SUPERINTENDENT when a sudden thought stayed his hand. It was not the kind of thought a conscientious, rule-abiding police officer would harbor for a moment. The lieutenant, however, was fully aware he had no business working on a closed case to begin with—and when you're breaking one set of rules, you might as well break them all.

He rang four of the other bells before the lock on the inner door began to click. Pushing it open, he waited until a female voice floated down the stairs. "Who is it?"

"Police Department, ma'am. You folks own that green Buick parked out in front?" There was no Buick, green or otherwise, along the street curbing, but Kirk figured she wouldn't know that.

"Why, no. Officer. I can't imagine—"

"Okay. Sorry we bothered you, lady," Kirk let the door swing into place hard enough to be heard upstairs. But this time he was on the right side of it.

There was a moment of silence, then he caught the sound of retreating feet and a door closed. Without waiting further, the Lieutenant mounted the stairs to the third floor, his feet soundless on the carpeted treads.

The entrance to 3C was secured by a tumbler-type lock. From an inner pocket Kirk took out a small flat leather case and a thin-edged tool from that. Working with the smooth efficiency of the expert, he loosened the door moulding near the lock and inserted the tool blade until it found the bolt. This he eased back, turned the door handle and, a moment later, was standing in a small living room tastefully furnished in modern woods.

His first action was to enter the tiny kitchen and unbolt the door leading to the rear porch. In case Alma Dakin arrived at an inopportune moment, he could be halfway down the outer steps while she was still engaged with the front door lock. Since he had pressed the moulding back into place, there would be nothing to indicate his presence.

Within ten minutes Kirk had ransacked every inch of the living room in search of something, anything, that would point to Alma Dakin as being more than a nine-to-five secretary. And while he found nothing, no one, not even the girl who lived here, could tell that an intruder had been at work.

The bedroom seemed even less promising at first. Dresser drawers gave up only the pleasantly personal articles of the average young woman. Miss Dakin, it turned out, was almost indecently fond of frothy undergarments and black transparent nightgowns—interesting but not at all important to the over-all problem.

Kirk, his search completed, sat down on the edge of the bed's footboard and totaled up what he had learned. It didn't take long, for he knew absolutely no more about Alma Dakin than he had before entering her apartment. No personal papers, no letters from a yearning boyfriend in the old home town, no savings or checking-account passbook. Not even a scrawled line of birthday or Christmas greetings on the fly leaves of the apartment's seven books.

To Kirk's trained mind, the very lack of such things, the fact that Alma Dakin lived in a vacuum, was highly significant. It smacked of her having something to hide— and his already strong suspicion of her was solidified into certainty of her guilt. But certainty was a long way from rock-ribbed evidence—and that was something he must have to proceed further.

He was ready to leave when it dawned on him that he had not yet looked under the bed. Kneeling, he pushed up the hanging edge of the green batik spread and peered into the narrow space. Nothing, not even a decent accumulation of dust. The light from the window was too faint, however, to reach a section of the floor near the footboard. Kirk climbed to his feet and attempted to shove that end to one side.

The bed failed to move. He blinked in mild surprise and tried again. It was only by exerting almost his entire strength that he was able to shift the thing at all, and then no more than a few inches.

He felt his pulse stir with the thrill of incipient discovery. Once he made sure nothing was anchoring the bed to the floor, he began to tap lightly against the wood in an effort to detect a possible false panel.

Within two minutes he located an almost microscopic crack in the headboard cleverly concealed by a decorative design running along the base. He ran his fingers lightly along the carvings until they encountered a small projection which gave slightly under pressure.

Kirk pressed down harder on the knob. A tiny *click* sounded against the silence and a section of wood some three feet square swung out. Lifting it aside, the detective found himself staring at an instrument board of some kind with a series of buttons and dials countersunk into it. The board itself formed a part of what was obviously a machine of some sort which evidently contained its own power, for there seemed to be no lead-in cord for plugging into a wall socket.

It could, Kirk thought, be a short wave radio transmitter. If it was, it looked like none he had ever come across before. On the other hand it could be some sort of infernal machine, ready to blow half the city to bits at the turn of a dial.

Even as his mind was weighing the advisability of tampering with the thing, his fingers were reaching for the various controls. Gingerly he moved one or two of the dials but nothing happened. A little more boldly now, he began to depress the buttons. As the third sank in, a low humming sound began to fill the room. Before Kirk could find a cut-off switch of some kind, the faint light of day streaming through the room's one window winked out, plunging him into a blackness so infinitely deep that it was like being buried alive.

Nothing can plunge a man into the sheerest panic like the absence of light. Even a man like Martin Kirk, who had walked almost daily with danger for the past fifteen years. And since the form panic takes varies with the individual, the Lieutenant's reaction was an utter inability to move so much as a finger.

Abruptly the low humming note ceased entirely, replaced immediately by the sound of a human voice. "Mythox. Contact established. Proceed."

Almost as though the words had tripped a lever in his brain, Kirk's paralysis ended. Both his hands seemed to swoop of their own volition to the invisible control panel and their fingers danced across the dials and buttons.

"Mythox," said the voice again. It seemed to swell and recede, like a direct radio newscast from half around the world. "Contact estab—"

The word ended as though it had run into a wall. The humming note came back, then ceased—and without warning daylight from the window washed over the bewildered and thoroughly frightened police officer.

Not until five minutes had passed was Martin Kirk sufficiently in control of his nervous system to even attempt replacing the loose panel in the headboard. When at last he managed to do so, he returned the bed to its original position, closed and bolted the kitchen door, took one last look around to make sure nothing was out of place, then slunk out of the apartment.

By the time he was back behind the wheel of his car and had burned up half a cigar, Kirk's brain was ready to function with something like its normal ability. He sat limp as Satan's collar, trying to piece together the significance of the last half hour's events.

There was no longer any doubt that Alma Dakin was in this mess up to her bangs. Linked as she was to the murders (and Kirk was convinced heart disease had nothing to do with it) of those scientists, he would have sworn she was a foreign agent bent on weakening America's defenses. Except for one thing. That machine. The kind of mind that could design and put together a mechanism like that was not of this planet. No longer did Paul Cordell's story of a girl who floated in a ball of blue fire sound like the ravings of a deranged brain. And the seeming miracle of Naia North's escape from a cell block now passed from fantasy to the factual.

What to do about it? Martin Kirk, at this moment undoubtedly the most bewildered man alive, put his head in his hands and tried to reach a decision. Take his story to the Police Commissioner? It would mean a padded cell—and without even bothering to see if Alma Dakin possessed a machine more complicated than an electric iron. Some government agency? By the time the red tape was unsnarled the former secretary could have reached Pakistan on foot.

Slowly from the depths of his terror of the Unknown, Martin Kirk's training in police procedure began to make itself felt. A plan started to form—hazy at first, then in a sharp and orderly pattern.

He left the car and returned to the apartment building. A glimpse of his badge and a few incisive orders masked as requests reduced the superintendent to a state of almost obsequious co-operation. Nor was the tenant of apartment 3D, a middle-aged spinster, any less anxious to assist the law. It seemed she had an older sister living on the other side of town who would be happy to put her up for a few days. She departed within the hour, a traveling bag in one fist.

Before that hour was gone, Chenowich, in response to a sizzling phone call, skidded a department car to a stop at the curb a block from the building. He delivered a dictograph to his superior, listened to a grim warning to keep his mouth shut about this at Headquarters, asked a couple of questions that drew no answers, and departed as swiftly as he had come.

The next step was the dangerous one. The superintendent admitted Kirk to the Dakin apartment and went down to the foyer to ring the bell in case the girl arrived at the wrong time. He soothed the Lieutenant's anxiety somewhat by explaining that she seldom returned to the place before seven o'clock, over three hours from now, but Kirk was taking no chances.

By five o'clock he had Alma Kirk's bedroom bugged and the instrument in working order and thoroughly tested. He was painstaking about removing all traces of plaster and sawdust and bits of wires before pushing the dresser back into place to cover the dictograph's receiver.

He found the superintendent stiffly on guard in the foyer and gave him his final instructions. The man listened respectfully, repeated them back to Kirk to convince him there would be no slip-up, and the Lieutenant went back upstairs to 3D to take up his vigil.

He was in the spinster's bedroom, working out a crossword puzzle, earphones in place, when he heard the sound of the bedroom door closing in the next apartment.

The time was 7:18.

CHAPTER SIX

It was like being in her room with his eyes shut. The soft scraping of drawers opening and closing, the creak of a chair being sat in, the cushioned thump of shoes dropped to the carpeted floor, even the rustle of a nylon slip as she drew it over her head.

It seemed much too early for her to turn in for the night. Was he going to be forced to sit there and listen to twelve of fourteen hours of feminine snoring? It would be damned unlikely in view of what was a cinch to be running through her mind.

Minutes later he heard her leave the bedroom, followed at once by the muted roar of a running shower. After that had lasted a normal length of time, the sound ceased and naked feet were audible on the bedroom rug. There was more opening and closing of drawers, the whisper of clothing being donned, and an irregular clicking sound like tapping glass against glass which he finally interpreted as part of the ritual of alternately combing and brushing hair while in front of the glass-topped vanity.

If there was anything of a panicky nature in her movements it would take better ears than his to detect it. But for Alma Dakin to get away with her kind of job required the nerves of lion trainer no matter what pressures she was subjected to.

Kirk stretched his legs, dug a cigar from the breast pocket of his coat and got it burning, then went back to the crossword puzzle with half his attention, keeping alert for any significant sound from the other apartment. His years as a minion of the law had adequately conditioned him to the utter boredom that went with the ordinary stake-out.

Several times the subject left the bedroom, but he was able to pick up sounds familiar enough to trace as emanating from the living room or kitchen. But nothing she did was worthy of notice in the home-town paper or even on the margin of a police blotter.

At 9:24 Alma Dakin again entered the bedroom. A hunch, or a sixth sense, or whatever years of experience in a single field gives a man, told Kirk that this time something would pop. He put aside the newspaper, placed a sheet of blank paper on the cover of a historical romance lifted from the spinster's nightstand, and got out a pencil.

A motor whined unexpectedly from the opposite side of the apartment wall and he could hear a heavy object roll with well-oiled smoothness a short distance across the carpet. He decided it was the bed being moved out from the wall by mechanical means rather than muscle, and it was clear to him now how she was able to get at that hidden radio, or whatever it was.

For the second time that day Kirk heard that eerie humming—a sound, he realized, that ordinarily would have been completely inaudible beyond the girl's bedroom walls. Suddenly the hum was chopped off and a familiar voice spoke familiar words.

"Mythox. Contact established. Proceed."

"A message for Orin. Alma Dakin."

A series of almost undetectable clicking sounds; then:

"Alma?" Despite the fact that the voice was coming through an amplifier, there was no distortion. "Anything wrong?"

It was a man's voice, clear, vibrant, young, and with no trace of an alien accent. Kirk's theory of an interplanetary menace lost some of its strength.

"I—I'm not sure, Orin," the girl said hesitantly. "There was a policeman at my apartment today—the same one Naia went to: The building superintendent told me."

"That's odd. There's no way *you* can be tied in with her. Or is there?"

"Not that I know of, Orin. Unless they've decided to check back on me just for the sake of something to do. If that's what's happened and they've learned I was working for Dr. Karney at the time of *his* death, they may get an idea the three deaths are related. And once a police officer gets suspicious, he can hound you unmercifully. That's what worries me, Orin. You know I'm not really an accomplished liar!"

"Shall we bring you here? At least long enough to build you a new identity?"

A pause. Then the girl's voice again: "Something else puzzles me, too. There's no mention of Naia's confession in the newspapers."

"*What?* You mean they haven't released Cordell? What will Tamu say?"

"If they have, nobody knows about it. I told you Naia should have remained in their hands until the young man was set free. You don't know my people as I do, Orin—none of you do."

"But the evidence? Nobody, not even the most stupid of Earthmen, could have ignored that evidence! Tamu won't like this."

"I can't help it, Orin. I keep telling you, Orin: you must use a new set of standards for this world. If its people thought as yours do, none of these unpleasant things would have to happen."

Another pause before the man's voice came over Kirk's earphones. "We didn't dare leave Naia in their hands. That's why we brought her back here. Look at the chance we took by permitting them to hold her even briefly. If only she hadn't blundered in the first place..."

His voice trailed off, then came back suddenly brisk. "Well, too late for regrets. We won't risk letting them question you. Field Seven in, say, three hours. Time enough?"

"More than enough!" Her relief was unmistakable. "It'll be wonderful visiting Mythox again, Orin. I hope Methu will allow me to stay for a long time."

"I hope so too, darling. But our work comes first; none of us dares let down for even a moment... See you soon. And don't neglect to eliminate the contrabeam."

"It will be gone seconds after we break contact. Field Seven at—let's see—12:30."

"I'll be there. Farewell, Alma."

The dim humming came back again, followed briefly by no sound at all. Then there was the noise of drawers being opened and closed with a kind of brisk and cheerful haste. Alma Dakin was preparing to take it on the lam!

Martin Kirk knew he had only a limited time to plan his own course of action. One way was to walk into the adjoining apartment, place Alma Dakin under arrest and force the whole story from her. A moment's reflection, however, caused him to abandon the idea. Any such move would end his chances of getting his hands on Naia North. More than anything else he wanted her, and he closed his mind to the broader aspects of what had taken—and was still taking—place.

No, his job was to follow Alma Dakin to her rendezvous with this man Orin and in some way force the two of them into turning Naia North over to him. This time she'd stick around long enough to stand trial—even if he had to handcuff her to the bars of her cell!

From beyond the wall he caught the sounds of suitcases being snapped shut, followed by the fading echo of footsteps. He jerked the earphones from his head and went quickly to the hall door in time to catch a glimpse of Alma Dakin on her way to the building stairs, a bulging suitcase in each hand.

Kirk raced for the kitchen of 3D, flung open the door and went down the rear steps with astonishing agility. He was opening the door of his car by the time the girl came out of the front entrance. He watched her place the bags in the trunk of a small sand-colored coupe, then slip in behind its wheel and start the motor.

The coupe passed his parked car, turned the corner and disappeared. Before it had reached the next intersection, Kirk was rolling smoothly half a block to her rear.

Two hours later both cars were moving along a winding country road miles from civilization. Kirk was driving without lights, bad enough under favorable circumstances but sheer folly considering the sky was completely overcast, so that he was denied even the faint radiance of the stars. Fortunately there was no other traffic in this desolate section at eleven o'clock at night, so that his only danger was in failing to remain on the twisting road.

Finally, near the crest of a particularly steep hill, two flaring red lights warned him his quarry was applying the brakes of her car. He cut his engine long enough to hear the coupe's motor die, then he swung his wheel to the right and coasted to a halt on the soft shoulder of the road.

Under cover of bushes and trees, naked of foliage at this time of the year, Kirk worked his way silently ahead until he could make out the dim figure of the girl as she dragged the pair of bags from the boot. Without a backward glance, she turned away from the road and an instant later was lost to sight among the trees.

There was nothing of the frontiersman in Lieutenant Martin Kirk, but fortunately the same was true of Alma Dakin. Where anyone accustomed to moving across natural terrain could have lost the officer with ease, in her case he need only pause briefly from time to time and use his ears.

At last the seemingly interminable forest ended and the girl sank wearily down on an upended suitcase. Kirk, perspiring freely under the folds of his topcoat, halted in the shelter of a tree bole, and waited.

Beyond where the girl sat was a large natural clearing covered with a fringe of winter grass. The silence was close to being absolute; only the faint keening of a chill wind and the restless creak of barren branches kept it from becoming unbearable.

Gradually his eyes became more and more accustomed to the absence of light worthy of the name, and he began to identify objects as something more than formless shadows. Alma Dakin appeared to be much closer to him than he had realized. He eyed her slim back malevolently, and when she lighted a cigarette, the wind bringing the odor of tobacco to his nostrils, he could cheerfully have strangled her for adding to his torture.

Time crawled by. An hour by reckoning was ten minutes by the illuminated dial of his wristwatch. His leg muscles began to twitch under the strain of holding the same position. Twice he managed to hold at bay explosive sneezes; he worried at being able to do so again.

The last five minutes before 12:30 was like being broken on the rack. He caught himself straining his ears for the sound of a motor, of a faint humming—of anything to indicate Orin was arriving. Nothing—and at 12:30 still nothing.

Martin Kirk had had all he could take. He was through standing out on a windy hill like some goddam—

Something seemed to flicker in the night air above the clearing—and he was staring slackjawed at a circular structure the size of a small house standing in the center of the clearing as though it had been there for years.

Before the Lieutenant could get his jaw off his necktie, Alma Dakin had uttered a cry of relief and was racing toward the nearest edge of the gleaming vessel. A panel in its side slid noiselessly back and the tall figure of a man was outlined in the opening.

"Alma!" he shouted and sprang to the ground to meet her.

They came together almost violently midway between the clearing's edge and the ship. She clung to him as he bent his head to meet her lips.

Kirk glanced past them at the open portal. Dim light from within cast a soft glow against the night. Nothing moved in the narrow segment of the interior visible from where he was standing.

And Kirk had a moment of what was as close to fear as he was able to know. A little time of bewilderment when his guard slipped just a trifle. What in the hell *was* all this? Into his solid world had come strange and unreasonable things. Crazy ships, and people who didn't play according to the rules he had learned over thankless drudging years as an honest cop. A few tiny beads of sweat formed on his upper lip.

Then his stubborn, inherent fatalism came to his aid. He grinned without humor. The hell with it. Whatever came up—a screwball flying saucer or a berserk psycho waving a gun. You played it the same; according to your own rules. This thing, whatever it was, bridged the gap to a killer. And when you found such a bridge, you crossed it.

Martin Kirk, his gun clutched tightly, moved like a casual shadow, eased his way along the hull of ship and slipped inside.

He had never seen anything like this. The lighting for one thing. It came from nowhere and somehow the stuff had a mood. It seemed alive—an intelligent force watching him, mocking him, sneering at him. And so potent was the mood of the whole setup, so sharp his need of release that he muttered, "The hell with you," and softly followed a circular corridor which curved off the hull.

They were coming toward the ship, Orin and Alma—coming while he still hunted a hole. He kept on going. If he met anybody they were going to go down. But he didn't. He found a steel stairway and a pocket at its base to hold his body. It wasn't a dark pocket. Light was everywhere. But the stairway hid him and the pair passed by and went on down the corridor.

He realized his right hand was aching and relaxed his grip on the gun butt he clutched. He straightened up and the tense little mirthless grin played on his lips.

Okay. Now where was she and how did it work? Could he find her and haul her off that silly tilt-a-whirl? He thought not. Either his eyes were bad or this thing had appeared from nowhere. Something inside snapped: Quit thinking that way! Whatever it looked like—*think right*. Follow the rules. Look for the dame. His grin deepened.

Sure.

He started walking. Around the eerie corridor in the direction opposite that taken by Orin and Alma Dakin. He walked a long time and there were no doors or anything else so the only thing to do was keep walking. He thought: When I come to that stairway I'll be back where I started but where's that? What good is a hall you keep going around and around in?

The ship lurched and threw him to the floor. It was going somewhere.

But it didn't go anywhere. Of that he was sure. Maybe he'd been fooled but it seemed the ship settled back after that single lurch and lay there like a choice segment out of someone's pet nightmare. Kirk got to his feet and rubbed the place his leg had violently met the floor.

He walked on and there was the steel stairway again and it was all very damned silly because he knew he'd circled the ship at least three times.

But lucky because the footsteps sounded again and as he dived toward the pocket, the wall of the ship opened to form a doorway. They forgot something, he thought. What kind of supermen are these? They can build a ship that has a stairway every third trip around and still they go away and forget things.

The grin was tighter than ever. Whistle in the dark, boy, but admit it—you're scared. Sure, but what's that got to do with it?

Orin and Alma left the ship. Martin Kirk pushed his head around the staircase. He crouched for sometime, staring through the open segment of the hull at the outside world. And his poor stupid orthodox mind asked a pitifully logical question:

How could it get light, with the sun at high noon, in fifteen minutes?

After a long, motionless time, the silence became such a roaring thing in Kirk's ears he could stand it no longer. He got up and walked to the doorway.

Something had gone somewhere; either the ship or the world he'd known, because out there was a different world and he knew damn well he'd never seen it before.

CHAPTER SEVEN

Martin Kirk stepped out into a circle of lush vegetation. And in doing so, he learned something. He learned that the human mind is a far more adaptable mechanism than most people imagine; that they can pelt you with goof balls and you get sweat on your lip and have to talk to yourself to keep from sliding off your rocker, but after a while when your mind seems halfway over the edge, it straightens up suddenly and starts going along. A defense mechanism against insanity? He didn't know.

He only knew that when the tiger roared, he whirled around with his gun leveled, saw the six-inch teeth, got wholesomely and sanely scared, and then everything was all right. He knew he was all right when he got the right reaction from sight of the almost naked girl holding the tiger.

For a long moment it was a frozen-action tableau. The huge orange and black beast. The wide-eyed young brunette nudist, and the tropical forest with the great big fat sun overhead. The girl's voice nailed it all down. "Don't be afraid. Rondo won't hurt you."

Kirk's resentment flared warmly and, had resentment been a tangible thing, he would have kissed it. "You're tootin' right he won't, sister. This isn't a toy I'm holding."

"Rondo is very gentle."

Kirk eyed the girl. "Why don't you put some clothes on?"

Her teeth were as bright and even as little white knives but her smile took the edge off them. "Only people in the city wear clothes. I wear them when I'm in the city. When I come out here I—"

"—you don't wear any clothes. Tell me—where am I?"

"Don't you know?"

"Let's not play games. If I knew I wouldn't ask you."

"Did you come on the ship?"

"You saw me get out of it didn't you? Now answer my question." And he realized how certain he was of what her answer would be.

"On Mythox."

"Well fancy that. Now tell me something else. Do you know what language you're speaking?"

"Of course. English."

"And why should you speak English on Mythox? Haven't you got a language of your own?"

"Certainly. But you're obviously from Earth. I thought you were a Watcher. I tried English. If you hadn't responded I'd have spoken to you in the other Earth languages."

"How many do you know?"

"Eleven hundred and seventeen. With various dialects, four thousand and—"

"There aren't that many."

She looked puzzled. Then her face cleared. "Oh you mean Earth languages. I was referring to those of the Five Galaxies."

I'm not going to be surprised at anything, he told himself doggedly. Not at anything. "Do you know anyone named Naia North?"

There was a childlike seriousness in her manner. It tended to deny the maturity of her body. Or was it the other way around? Martin Kirk wasn't sure, and grimly assured himself that he didn't give a damn.

The girl said, "I don't know anyone by that name. But I could find her for you."

"How would you go about it?"

"I'd go to the city and check the video-directory, naturally."

"Naturally. And you'd put your clothes on before you went?"

"Of course I would. We go without clothing only out here in the playground."

Kirk realized he'd been holding the gun rigidly in front of him. The tiger had dropped to the ground and lay outstretched like a lazy, good-natured dog. Kirk lowered the gun, setting his eyes again on the girl. "A minute ago you said you thought I was a Watcher. What did you mean?"

He would have framed his questions with more guile, but something told him it wasn't necessary. This child of nature was utterly without guile. She said, "An Earth Watcher. What did you think I meant?"

"I didn't know or I wouldn't have asked."

It clarified. *Dakin is watching.* Sure. What the hell else would a Watcher do but watch? But why, and for what? Kirk was mystified. But it didn't matter, he asserted inwardly, and turned his mind back to the straight line. The cop's line. "Will you put on your clothes and go into the city and locate Naia North for me?"

"If it will help you."

"It will. Where can I wait for you?"

"If you want to see Naia North why don't you come with me?"

Kirk shrugged. Why not? So long as the score was completely unknown to him, why not follow the path of least resistance? "Get your clothes on," he said.

The girl turned and started leading the tiger back toward a grove of trees. After a few steps she turned back, a look of sober thought on her face. "Are all Earthlings so assertive?" she asked. Kirk grinned. As long as it works, this one is, baby. But what if it stops working? His reply was not audible and the girl turned finally to disappear into the bushes.

Kirk then experienced a strange feeling of unreality which persisted until the girl returned.

"My name is Raima," the girl said solemnly. She wore tight-fitting trousers, a loose blouse and had a silver colored air car with room in back for the tiger.

Kirk knew it was an air car when the craft lifted from the ground from no apparent means of acceleration and skimmed along just above the trees. He sat beside Raima and asked, "About that ship I came here in? How fast does it travel and how far is it from Mythox to Earth?"

"The distance is around two hundred thousand light years but the ship doesn't really travel at all."

"Maybe you could go into a little more detail," Kirk said wearily.

"It's very simple. Distance, as you Earthlings regard it, is not distance at all. Space bends to a greater or lesser degree depending upon its immediate function in whatever time-space equation you are using."

"Thank you very much," Kirk replied and silently added: Keep to the line. Hold to your own values. On Earth, wherever it is, a man is waiting to go to the chair for a murder he didn't commit. Use whatever equation you want to—that still adds up the same. These people may be a lot smarter than you are, but they can't twist that one and make you believe it comes out any different.

A strange city of graceful flying spirals was coming over the horizon. It moved closer and the air car arced in to a halt on a huge cement landing area punctuated with small circles of a different material.

Raima jumped from the cockpit and Kirk followed to hear the soft thud of the cat's four paws landing beside him. The cat went over and sat down on one of the circles. Raima followed, stood beside the animal and called, "Don't you want to go down to street level?"

"Of course. How stupid of me not to know how."

The circle dropped silently beneath them in a bright metal tube in which a door soon appeared to let them out into a broad street filled with casually moving pedestrians. Kirk noted that none of them seemed in any hurry; that here and there was an individual dressed like himself. Watchers on furlough or vacation, he thought a trifle bitterly. This picture was far from complete but enough of it added up to furnish a name for them. Quizling was a good one. Perhaps traitor was better.

All in all, he found one satisfaction. He could travel about as he pleased.

A short walk brought them to a huge four or five story wall, the like of which Kirk had never seen. It was symmetrically covered with small, opaque, glass windows, beside each of which was a dial not unlike the ones on Earth telephones. Catwalks of some bright metal covered the wall. On these catwalks, numerous people were busy with a strange business Kirk could not follow.

"This is the video-directory," Raima said. She gave no further explanation, but while Rondo lazily rubbed noses with a bear cub sitting on its haunches waiting for its master, she spun the dial with practiced efficiency. "Now, if Naia North is in the city and wishes to see you, her image will appear in the mirror."

As Kirk watched and the bear slapped the grinning tiger with a playful paw, the opaque glass cleared and the tall, willowy figure of Naia North appeared in miniature.

"You may speak in here," Raima said, solemnly indicating a small screened opening beside the mirror. "My! She's pretty, isn't she?"

Naia North was entirely composed. She wore a pale blue gown and from the background in the mirror, Kirk gathered that she was at home. "Aren't you surprised?" Kirk asked.

Now a slight frown creased the lovely Naia's brow. "A little perhaps. How did you get to Mythox? And why did you come?"

"A slight matter of murder. A murder you confessed to, or has it slipped your mind?"

"Aren't you being rather absurd? That's all done with."

"Not so far as Paul Cordell is concerned. He's going to the chair—only he isn't. We're going back and straighten a few things out."

Genuine surprise was reflected now. And possibly a certain contempt. "My opinion of you lessens. I hadn't rated you as a complete fool. How did you get here?"

"The same way you did I suppose, is there more than one way?"

Naia's frown deepened. "Do you mean you were *brought*—?"

"Not intentionally, I stowed away on that funny round ship that doesn't go anywhere and travels far."

The beautiful brow immediately cleared. "Oh, I see," Naia observed with amusement. "And you know exactly how you'll get me back to Earth I suppose? Thousands of light years. It's a long walk."

"I'll take one thing at a time and worry about them in order of appearance. The main thing for you to remember, is this: You may be as smart as all get out but you broke an American law on American soil by your own confession and by God you're going back and answer for it!"

"Idiot! I can have you—"

Kirk's mood changed to the quizzical. "It's entirely beside the point, but still I don't get you, baby. Why the switcheroo? You walked in and confessed. Then you took a powder. Now you sneer in my teeth. What do you use for a rudder, sweetheart?"

"I followed orders," Naia flared with a mixture of anger and sullenness. "I am now free of the assignment."

Kirk pursed his lips thoughtfully. "You wouldn't be sort of a hatchet-woman for this high-blown outfit, would you? I can think offhand of a few other names. Karney, Blatz, Kennedy. What gives with knocking off nuclear physicists, baby?"

Naia did not answer. When she started to turn away from the mirror, Kirk glanced at the silent Raima standing with her hand on the tiger's head. "Is there any way I can call on the lady in the mirror personally?"

"Not if she doesn't want to receive you," Raimu said. She was studying Kirk, with wistful dark eyes.

Naia turned back quickly. "I'll be glad to receive you. It's time I taught you a lesson."

"Fine. What's your address?"

But Naia was gone. The little mirror turned opaque. Kirk shot a questioning glance at Raimu. "Does yes mean no on this cockeyed planet?"

"Her car will come." Raima murmured. But the petite dark beauty seemed interested in other things. "You didn't tell me your name."

"Sorry. Rude of me. It's Martin Kirk. You've been pretty nice to me. I wish there was some way I could show my appreciation."

"You're going to see Naia North?"

"Yes. She's a murderess. I'm taking her back to my planet."

"I'm afraid that wouldn't be possible."

"You too, honey?" Kirk reached out and flicked one of the raven curls. "If things were different you and I might be able to have fun."

"I spend a lot of time—where you found me. Maybe—"

"I doubt if I can make it. But keep your clothes on after this—as a personal favor to me."

She was the very soul of solemnity. "I don't understand you. I really don't understand you at all."

At that moment, an air car—much smaller than Raima's, dropped gently into the street beside Kirk. "Good lord! Did this thing smell me out?"

"It came to the mirror on Naia's private wave-length. Get in. It will take you to her."

Kirk crawled into the car. The last thing he saw before it lifted into the air, were Raima's dazzling black eyes. The last words he heard were, "Goodbye, Martin Kirk. I will visualize you."

The car swung up above the graceful, spidery buttresses and moved across the city. Kirk filled in the time by trying to figure out what made the thing go. He hadn't gotten to first base when the car lost altitude and came to rest on a balcony hung with seeming perilousness on a sheer white wall. Kirk stepped out. A large glass panel had been pushed back and Naia stood waiting in the opening.

"Nice of you to receive me," Kirk said. "Have you got your bags packed for a trip stateside?"

"Please come this way."

Naia turned and moved through the room just off the balcony. On the far side another door gave exit. She passed through it and turned as though waiting for Kirk. He took one step, two, three, four.

Then something came from somewhere and almost tore his jaw off. He went out in an explosion of black light.

CHAPTER EIGHT

Kirk came to with the feeling that his period of unconsciousness had been momentary. Naia was standing as she had stood before, just beyond the inner doorway. The mocking smile was still on her face. "Did you trip?"

Kirk got groggily to his feet. "No, angel. That's the way I always cross a room." As he came upright his hand reached toward the bulge made by his shoulder holster. But it didn't get that far.

He had not seen from whence the first blow came but that was not true with the second. From a tiny opening in the door jamb, a pinpoint of light appeared. It hung there for a moment. Then it brightened, expanded, and shot forth as a slim beam. It contained a silvery radiance and the kick of a Missouri mule. It slammed against Kirk's jaw, but not quite so hard this time; only hard enough to send him down again amidst a cloud of shooting stars.

He shook his head and got to his hands and knees. "Wha's 'at? A trained flashlight?" He began coming up. As soon as he didn't need his right hand for rising he reached for his gun. The light beam seemed to resent this. It hit him in the solar plexus this time; a sickening blow that fed nausea down through his legs. He tightened his stomach against the agony and began getting up again.

"You see how useless it is?" Naia asked. "Beside us, you Earthlings are children. Will you stop being foolish, or must I kill you?"

Kirk squinted craftily at the pinpoint of light with one closed eye. Clever little devil. What the hell! Nude innocents. Tigers on leashes. Light beams that knocked your teeth out. Paul Cordell with a shaved spot on his head.

"You got your bag packed for a little trip, baby?"

For a brief moment, genuine fear flamed in Naia's eyes. And in Kirk's mind: Dumb babe. What's she got to be scared of? They hit you with nothing and make it stick. Kirk croaked, "Grab your bag, baby. We'll go find that flying biscuit. We got a date with Arthur Kahler Troy."

He was really cagey this time. When the light beam shot out, he hurled himself to the side. But he could have saved the effort. A beam came from the other door jamb and he stepped right into it. That one really tore his head off.

Somebody was talking. It was a man and he had a deep resonant voice: a voice full of authority—and censure. "I'm surprised at you Naia. I never suspected you of having a sadistic streak."

Naia's sullen reply. "Do you think anyone can do the work I do and remain unmarked?"

"I suppose not. But as I remember it, you asked to serve."

"As a benefit to humanity."

"We won't go into it."

But Naia pressed the point. "I have always followed orders. I placed myself in possible jeopardy on Earth by clearing Paul Cordell."

"But Paul Cordell was not cleared."

"Not through any fault of mine."

"But why this? What end does torturing this poor unfortunate serve?"

Martin Kirk cautiously opened one eye. It brought to his brain the image of a large blue globe. A man of fine and commanding appearance stood within the globe, suspended about a foot from the floor. The globe and the man gave every indication of having just come through the opaque glass wall of the room, and as Kirk watched, the man was lowered slowly to the floor and the globe became a blue mist that spiralled lazily and was gone.

Kirk opened both eyes now, stirred, and climbed dizzily to his feet. "You bump into the damndest things around here," he said, "But let's get down to the important business. My name is Martin Kirk. I'm an American police officer. One of your subjects committed a murder on American soil. I hope you aren't going to be difficult about extradition."

The other could not hide his surprise. Nor did he try to. "Amazing," he murmured. Then, "I am Tamu, the overlord of the galaxy. I wonder if Naia's cruelty hasn't affected your mind?"

"If you mean I'm nuts, I think maybe you're right. But it wasn't little Playful here who did it. I've gone through a lot and I don't speak with any sense of bragging. I've seen more funny things happen than any one man should see in so short a time. So maybe I am off my rocker. So I'd like your permission to take my prisoner back to Earth so I can give all my time to regaining my sanity."

Tamu regarded Kirk with thoughtful eyes. "I think we should have a talk."

"I would like a talk. I would like nothing better than to chew the fat with you for hours on end if my jaw didn't hurt so damned much. So I'll just take my prisoner and go. Do I have to sign a paper or something?"

The overlord's surprise was fast becoming a kind of fascinated awe. "Kirk, you said?" He pointed to the door leading to the inner room. "Please go in, sir. There's no use of our standing out here while we discuss your problem."

The Lieutenant eyed the door frame warily, "I tried getting through there before but the light got in my eyes!"

"You can trust me."

The police officer stepped cautiously through the opening and on into a luxuriously furnished room. Tamu, dressed much the same as one of Earth's better bankers, followed him in and suggested he sit down.

"Why?" Kirk demanded bluntly. "Let's stop kitten-and-micing around, Mr. Tamu. I'm not comfortable here and I want to leave. With her." He tilted his head toward the watching, sullen-faced Naia North. "And now."

Tamu said, "Believe me, it will be as easy for you to return to Earth an hour from now. You seem weary to the point of exhaustion. I ask you again: sit down and get back some of your strength. Naia will find you something to eat."

Kirk's stubborn determination to force an immediate showdown wavered. It had been born largely of fear to begin with, and the thought of relief for his burning throat was impossible to resist.

"I could use a drink," he admitted.

Tamu gestured and Naia North turned to leave the room. But Kirk leaped forward to block her off. "Nothing doing! I don't take my eyes off you, baby. I'll just pass up that drink."

The girl glanced at the overlord and shrugged helplessly. Tamu said, "Have a girl bring in something. While we're waiting I suggest all three of us get comfortable."

While Naia was speaking into a tiny screen set into one of the silk-covered walls, Tamu and the man from Earth sat down across from each other on a pair of fragile-legged chairs. The overlord leaned back and sighed. "You've asked my leave to return to Earth and to take Naia back with you to stand trial for murder. Have you considered that I may refuse that permission?"

"I don't think I have to consider it," Kirk said promptly.

"You don't?" Tamu was mystified again. "Why not?"

"You tell me you're the overlord. I take that to mean you're in charge. That means you have laws to govern your people and *that* means you believe in laws. One of your subjects has broken the law of my country. You can't refuse to let her take the consequences any more than if the situation was reversed."

Tamu was shaking his head and smiling slightly. "I'm afraid you're not taking into consideration one fact, Mr. Kirk. Naia North broke your law, as you call it, on express and definite instructions from me."

Martin Kirk made a show of astonishment. "Let me get this straight. You *ordered* Professor Gilmore and Juanita Cordell murdered? Is that what you're telling me?"

"Yes."

"Why?"

"Exactly the reason I suggested we have a talk. To make you see why they—and others in the same classification— could not be allowed to live."

"Men like Karney? Kennedy? Blatz?"

Tamu blinked. "My respect for you increases, Martin Kirk."

"Don't let it throw you. I'm a police officer, and police officers are trained to do the job right."

The overlord crossed his legs and settled deeper into the chair. "Mythox needs men like you, Martin Kirk. That is why I'm going to give you a chance for life. For this you must understand: if I wanted it, you would be dead within seconds."

A chill slid along the stubborn back of the Lieutenant but nothing showed in his impassive expression and he did not speak.

"But because we do need you, I am going to tell you things no Earthman knows. I believe that once you understand why Mythox has undertaken to meddle in the affairs of another world—and I tell you frankly that our doing so is as abhorrent to us as anything you can imagine— once you understand our reasons, you will cheerfully, even eagerly, join us."

"And if I don't?"

"You know the answer to that, I'm sure."

A slim fair-haired girl in a pale green toga-like dress entered the room carrying a tray holding tall glasses of some sparkling blue beverage. She offered it first to Kirk, then the others. The Lieutenant removed one of the glasses, waited until Tamu and Naia had done the same, but not until they had drunk some of the liquid did he tilt his own glass. The cold tangy liquid hit him like a bombshell—a bombshell on the pleasant side. He could almost literally feel his strength flow back, his senses sharpen and the poisons of fatigue and mental strain disappear.

"I'm listening," he said.

Tamu set his glass on the edge of a nearby table and bent forward, his manner earnest. "It won't take long, Martin Kirk. Hear me. We of Mythox are far in advance of the peoples of Earth—both spiritually and scientifically. Life on our planet materialized in much the same manner as on your own world, but countless ages before. Almost the same process of evolution took place; but somewhere along the line humanity on Mythox managed to reach full development without the flaws of character found among so many of Earth's inhabitants. When I tell you that we find it almost impossible to voice an untruth, that taking a human life willfully for any reason is equally difficult, that crime of any nature is almost unknown here—then you will see the difference between the two planets.

"For ages our scientists have observed the events taking place on Earth. By perfecting a method for changing matter from terrene to contraterrene, we have managed to bridge the million light years of space separating our worlds as we saw fit. Thousands of years ago we could have gained control of your ball of clay and turned mankind into any pattern we might choose.

"That is not our way, Martin Kirk. Free will is our heritage too—and we respect it in ourselves, and for that reason must respect it in others. So long as Earth's peoples confined their more destructive tendencies to themselves we kept our hands off—even while we failed to understand such senseless conduct.

"And then one day we witnessed an explosion on Earth's surface—an explosion different from any of the countless ones before it. That explosion was the first man-made release of atomic energy—a process we had known how to bring about for ages, but one we would never use. For we have learned the secret of limitless power without the transformation of mass into energy. Your way is the way of destruction, Martin Kirk; ours is exactly the opposite.

"For the first time, the leaders of Mythox knew the meaning of fear—fear that, once Earth's scientists had found the secret of nuclear fission they would go on to the one extreme forbidden throughout the Universe itself.

"And so we acted. Not in the way your people would have acted were the situations reversed. For we were still determined that there would be no intervention on our part in Earth's affairs—and that is still our way, just as it must always be. But there must be one exception to this rule: no one on Earth must be allowed to blunder into the extreme I mentioned a moment ago."

Tamu, overlord of Mythox, paused to drink from his glass and to cast a speculative glance at the stolid face of Martin Kirk. He might as well have studied the contours of a brick wall.

"The road to that blunder had been opened the day your learned men first split the atom. If they persisted down that path, it was bound to follow that they would attempt the thing we feared: the splitting of hydrogen atoms—the hydrogen bomb, as you call it.

"We know what that would mean: a chain reaction that would wipe out an entire galaxy in one blinding flash. *Our galaxy*, Martin Kirk—yours and mine! Do you have any thought at all on what that means?"

The question was rhetorical; even before Kirk could shake his head, the overlord pressed on.

"Mythox and Earth are two grains of dust on opposite sides of a galaxy—a spiral formation of stars and planets 200,000 light years wide and 20,000 thick. Between us lie countless other worlds, a vast number of them supporting life—not always, or even often, life as we know it, but life nonetheless.

"There is not one of those worlds, Martin Kirk, we do not know as thoroughly as we do our own. Fortunately for our purpose only a relative few have progressed along a line which can lead to danger for the rest. Yours is one of those which has—and that is why we of Mythox have taken a well-masked place in your affairs *so far as they relate to nuclear physics.*

"Every scientist of your world, male or female, is constantly under the eye of a Watcher. These Watchers are members of your own races—people we have enlisted in the fight to save not just their world or mine—but millions of worlds.

"When a Watcher learns a physicist is close to the one key to success in his effort to make a hydrogen bomb—an equation that begins: 'Twelve times zero point seven nine'— we are notified and a killer from our own people is sent to execute that scientist. Yes, Martin Kirk, we have those among us—a very few—who are capable of killing on orders and for cause. Naia, here, is one of them. She was sent to take the lives of Gregory Gilmore and Juanita Cordell; but she bungled and instead of their deaths resembling heart failure, they were obviously murdered.

"Alma Dakin tried to cover up the truth by making it appear both scientists had died at the hands of a jealous husband. She succeeded, both because of her perjured testimony and the fact that Paul Cordell insisted on telling the truth. But when we of Mythox learned what had happened, Naia was sent back to confess the crime. She entered the laboratory only a few hours before she came to your office; while she was in the laboratory the second time, the clues you found were put there.

"Our mistake was in thinking that, once proof was offered clearing Cordell, the innocent man would be freed. For once more we credited Earthlings with the same code of ethics we of Mythox adhere to.

"You succeeded in following Naia here. Only a man composed of equal parts of Earth bulldog and genius could have done so. Martin Kirk, I offer you a place among us and a lifetime devoted to making sure the galaxy of which we both are a part does not perish. What say you?"

Several minutes dragged by. The eyes of both Tamu and Naia North were glued to the grim visage of Homicide Lieutenant Kirk. It was impossible for either of them to know what thoughts were churning behind that stone face.

Abruptly he stood up. "I'm a cop. I leave your kind of problem to the people who are good at it. My people, Tamu. You see, I belong to my world, not to yours.

"But you've got a solid argument—one I'd be a fool not to consider. Let me sleep on it. Tomorrow morning we'll talk about it some more; then I'll give you my answer. Right now I'm too worn out to think in a straight line."

"Of course." The overlord rose to his feet. "Find Martin Kirk comfortable quarters, Naia, and leave orders he is not to be disturbed until he is ready to join us."

On his way down a corridor behind the same slip of a girl who had brought him his drink, Martin Kirk was thinking: They didn't even frisk me for a gun!

Martin Kirk went into his apartment and lay for a while looking at the ceiling. After a time, he got up and went out again.

CHAPTER NINE

The soft silvery radiance, which this planet seemed to feature, bathed the metal hallway as Kirk marched stolidly toward the slim arcing stairway that led toward Naia's floor. This was certainly a strange building, he thought. The engineers of Mythox certainly knew how to use curves in their architecture. They utilized them for utility and beauty to a point where a straight line was something to be surprised at. Pretty smart people, the Mythoxians—in more ways than one.

And Kirk, for no apparent reason, thought of a phrase common among children back during his own childhood...

"Who died and left you boss?"

He counted the markings over one door. He had seen those markings before. Naia North lived here.

And Naia North was in. Kirk walked softly across the large foyer room and quietly pushed open a door to the left. Naia, clad as always, in beauty, lay sleeping on a bed that stood out from the wall on two narrow rods of metal and needed no other support.

As Kirk opened his mouth, Naia awakened, so she was looking calmly at him as he spoke. "Up, baby. You've got a date with a hot electrode a lot of light years from here. It's a hike, so rise and shine."

Naia sat up very slowly, very gracefully. She was what men dream of finding in bed beside them. What they marry to keep in bed beside them.

"You must be mad."

"As a hatter, baby. Into your duds."

He saw her glance at the door jamb of the bedroom entrance, saw the shadow of disappointment in her lovely eyes.

"You didn't put those Joe Louis light rays in your bedroom, did you?"

Naia set her feet on the floor and drew herself up to her full height. She wore a garment light blue in color, a gown that hung as had that of Guinevere, as that of the Maid of Shalot.

But Naia was contempt. She was contempt clothed in cold blue, then contempt naked as she allowed the gown to fall delicately to the floor. A few minutes later, she was contempt clothed for the street in tight britches and a loose blouse.

"You go first," Kirk said. "And do as you're told. You may be a Mythoxian, but this .45 doesn't know that. It puts big holes in anybody."

As Mala walked serenely toward the hall door, there was only a touch of sullenness at the corners of her mouth. She turned her head to speak over her shoulder. "Hiding behind a woman, brave Earthman?"

"Yes and no. I'm hiding behind a woman from those damn straight-left rays; and I'm not a brave Earthman. I spend most of my time scared to death. That's why all of us are getting back to Earth quick, so I can draw an easy breath."

"All of us?"

"Oh yes. Didn't I tell you? You're taking me to the places I can find Alma Dakin and Orin. We're going to have witnesses and testimony. And the party who gets burned isn't going to be Paul Cordell."

"I won't—"

"Hold it, honey."

Kirk had picked up two items upon leaving Naia's apartment. A pair of filmy silk stockings and a white scarf. He jerked Naia's hands behind her back in somewhat of a surprise move. Before she recovered, her wrists were tightly bound.

She gasped, "You—madman."

A moment later he deftly pulled the scarf across her mouth and twisted it into an effective gag. He stepped back to admire his handywork.

"Now we're all ready. Orin and Alma."

Naia shook her head in a slow negative, Kirk pushed her gently into the hall and rounded to face her.

"Yes," he said. "You ought to know now I won't be stopped. I need Orin to fly that space buggy. If I don't get him we can't go. Then there'd be nothing left for me to do but even the score for Paul Cordell. He'll have to go but you'll keep him company."

Naia stood like a statue, apparently considering the gravity of the situation. Then she made her way slowly down the corridor in the opposite direction from which Kirk had come. Down three curving flights and stopping finally in front of a door identical to her own. Kirk stepped forward and leaned firmly on the knob. The door opened. He knew where the bedroom was in these apartments now. He pushed Naia ahead of him, into the bedroom and saw Alma lying with her eyes closed.

Kirk whirled, just in time to level his gun and bring Orin to a dead stop. "Over by the bed, high-born." As Orin complied, Kirk leered at Naia. "That was clever, but I had it doped. I spotted them for husband and wife or the Mythox equivalent some time back. A good chance shot to hell."

"What do you want here?" Orin demanded.

"A chauffeur. We're heading Earthward on the first ship. That's the one out in the jungle."

"But you talked to Tamu. I thought—"

"I'd been suckered? No, no my friend! On the force they called me the boy with the one-track mind."

"I can see what they meant," Orin sighed.

"I thought you would. Tell your wife to get dressed. We're getting an air-sled."

"You might have the decency to—"

"I won't turn my back. You can stand between us. That's the best I can do."

Alma dressed swiftly in a costume similar to Naia's.

When they were ready to leave, Kirk said, "Now let's get it straight once and for all. I'll stand for no fast moves. It's Earth, or some quick slugs. Do you follow me?"

They did not speak but they evidently believed Kirk because, minutes later, the party of four stood beside the ugly ship while thick trees and grasses whispered around them.

"Inside."

In the corridor, Orin abruptly stopped for several seconds and turned as though having thought of a convincing argument he was bent upon trying. However, Kirk poked him sharply in the ribs with the barrel of the .45 and he moved on after the women toward the ladder and thence to the motor room.

Once inside, Orin turned and spoke sharply. "Won't you reconsider?"

"Push the levers, Jack. The right ones."

"Tamu is a reasonable man. We could talk to him again. He would make even a more generous offer."

"I'm waiting."

"Certainly you did not refute the logic of his argument? We are in the right. Our case is just. The galaxies must be protected from—"

"The right levers, Jack."

"—from those who through ignorance, stupidity, or ferocity would destroy it."

"One more minute of this and there'll be dead people aboard this ship."

"You're helpless, really. You can't fly this ship without me. Therefore my life is safe. I merely refuse to launch it."

"Would you like a dead wife?"

Orin whitened perceptibly.

"She may be a wife to you, but to me she's just a doll who helped lie a man into the chair."

"You wouldn't do it! You haven't got the nerve to shoot down a man or a woman...to shoot them down in cold blood."

Kirk looked steadily into Orin's eyes. "You don't believe that do you, bud?"

Orin held the gaze for a long time. After what seemed to be an eternity, he then dropped his eyes. "No...no I don't believe it."

"Then get to work."

"One last offer. Won't you reconsider. Join us?"

"No!"

"Very well."

And Orin, a fixed, taut look on his face, reached forth his hand and touched a button on the panel board. It was a very special button.

A button for use only when all hope was gone.

The exploding space-time ship lighted the countryside to blinding brilliance.

*   *   *

A.P. Jan 21ˢᵗ—Shortly after midnight today, Paul Cordell, convicted killer in the famous "woman from Mars" case, was put to death in the electric chair at the state penitentiary.

THE END

If you've enjoyed this book, you will not want to miss these terrific titles…

ARMCHAIR SCI-FI & HORROR DOUBLE NOVELS, $12.95 each

D-11 **PERIL OF THE STARMEN** by Kris Neville
THE FORGOTTEN PLANET by Murray Leinster

D-12 **THE STAR LORD** by Boyd Ellanby
CAPTIVES OF THE FLAME by Samuel R. Delaney

D-13 **MEN OF THE MORNING STAR** by Edmund Hamilton
PLANET FOR PLUNDER by Hal Clement and Sam Merwin, Jr.

D-14 **ICE CITY OF THE GORGON** by Chester S. Geier and Richard Shaver
WHEN THE WORLD TOTTERED by Lester Del Rey

D-15 **WORLDS WITHOUT END** by Clifford D. Simak
THE LAVENDER VINE OF DEATH by Don Wilcox

D-16 **SHADOW ON THE MOON** by Joe Gibson
ARMAGEDDON EARTH by Geoff St. Reynard

D-17 **THE GIRL WHO LOVED DEATH** by Paul W. Fairman
SLAVE PLANET by Laurence M. Janifer

D-18 **SECOND CHANCE** by J. F. Bone
MISSION TO A DISTANT STAR by Frank Belknap Long

D-19 **THE SYNDIC** by C. M. Kornbluth
FLIGHT TO FOREVER by Poul Anderson

D-20 **SOMEWHERE I'LL FIND YOU** by Milton Lesser
THE TIME ARMADA by Fox B. Holden

ARMCHAIR SCIENCE FICTION CLASSICS, $12.95 each

C-4 **CORPUS EARTHLING**
by Louis Charbonneau

C-5 **THE TIME DISSOLVER**
by Jerry Sohl

C-6 **WEST OF THE SUN**
by Edgar Pangborn

ARMCHAIR SCI-FI & HORROR GEMS SERIES, $12.95 each

G-1 **SCIENCE FICTION GEMS, Vol. One**
Isaac Asimov and others

G-2 **HORROR GEMS, Vol. One**
Carl Jacobi and others

If you've enjoyed this book, you will not want to miss these terrific titles…

ARMCHAIR SCI-FI & HORROR DOUBLE NOVELS, $12.95 each

D-21 **EMPIRE OF EVIL** by Robert Arnette
THE SIGN OF THE TIGER by Alan E. Nourse & J. A. Meyer

D-22 **OPERATION SQUARE PEG** by Frank Belknap Long
ENCHANTRESS OF VENUS by Leigh Brackett

D-23 **THE LIFE WATCH** by Lester Del Rey
CREATURES OF THE ABYSS by Murray Leinster

D-24 **LEGION OF LAZARUS** by Edmond Hamilton
STAR HUNTER by Andre Norton

D-25 **EMPIRE OF WOMEN** by John Fletcher
ONE OF OUR CITIES IS MISSING by Irving Cox

D-26 **THE WRONG SIDE OF PARADISE** by Raymond F. Jones
THE INVOLUNTARY IMMORTALS by Rog Phillips

D-27 **EARTH QUARTER** by Damon Knight
ENVOY TO NEW WORLDS by Keith Laumer

D-28 **SLAVES TO THE METAL HORDE** by Milton Lesser
HUNTERS OUT OF TIME by Joseph E. Kelleam

D-29 **RX JUPITER SAVE US** by Ward Moore
BEWARE THE USURPERS by Geoff St. Reynard

D-30 **SECRET OF THE SERPENT** by Don Wilcox
CRUSADE ACROSS THE VOID by Dwight V. Swain

ARMCHAIR SCIENCE FICTION CLASSICS, $12.95 each

C-7 **THE SHAVER MYSTERY, pt. 1**
by Richard S. Shaver

C-8 **THE SHAVER MYSTERY, pt. 2**
by Richard S. Shaver

C-9 **MURDER IN SPACE** by David V. Reed
by David V. Reed

ARMCHAIR MASTERS OF SCIENCE FICTION SERIES, $16.95 each

M-3 **MASTERS OF SCIENCE FICTION, Vol. Three**
Robert Sheckley, "The Perfect Woman" and other tales

M-4 **MASTERS OF SCIENCE FICTION, Vol. Four**
Mack Reynolds, "Stowaway" and other tales

If you've enjoyed this book, you will not want to miss these terrific titles...

ARMCHAIR SCI-FI & HORROR DOUBLE NOVELS, $12.95 each

D-41 **FULL CYCLE** by Clifford D. Simak
IT WAS THE DAY OF THE ROBOT by Frank Belknap Long

D-42 **THIS CROWDED EARTH** by Robert Bloch
REIGN OF THE TELEPUPPETS by Daniel Galouye

D-43 **THE CRISPIN AFFAIR** by Jack Sharkey
THE RED HELL OF JUPITER by Paul Ernst

D-44 **WE THE MACHINE** by Gerald Vance
PLANET OF DREAD by Dwight V. Swain

D-45 **THE STAR HUNTER** by Edmond Hamilton
THE ALIEN by Raymond F. Jones

D-46 **WORLD OF IF** by Rog Phillips
SLAVE RAIDERS FROM MERCURY by Don Wilcox

D-47 **THE ULTIMATE PERIL** by Robert Abernathy
PLANET OF SHAME by Bruce Elliot

D-48 **THE FLYING EYES** by J. Hunter Holly
SOME FABULOUS YONDER by Phillip Jose Farmer

D-49 **THE COSMIC BUNGLARS** by Geoff St. Reynard
THE BUTTONED SKY by Geoff St. Reynard

D-50 **TYRANTS OF TIME** by Milton Lesser
PARIAH PLANET by Murray Leinster

ARMCHAIR SCIENCE FICTION CLASSICS, $12.95 each

C-13 **THE SUNKEN WORLD**
by Stanton A. Coblentz

C-14 **THE LAST VIAL**
by Sam McClatchie, M. D.

C-15 **WE WHO SURVIVED (THE FIFTH ICE AGE)**
by Sterling Noel

ARMCHAIR MASTERS OF SCIENCE FICTION SERIES, $16.95 each

MS-5 **MASTERS OF SCIENCE FICTION, Vol. Five**
Winston K. Marks—Test Colony and other classics

MS-6 **MASTERS OF SCIENCE FICTION, Vol. Six**
Fritz Leiber—Deadly Moon and other classics

www.ingramcontent.com/pod-product-compliance
Lightning Source LLC
Chambersburg PA
CBHW050323200626
46810CB00022B/993